THE ADVENTURES OF

MAX AND MAUDE

JOHN LOSEE

Copyright
Copyright © 2021 by John Losee
All rights reserved. No part of this book may be reproduced, distributed or transmitted in any manner without written permission of the copyright owner.

Author's Note
This is a work of fiction. Names, characters, places and incidents are a product of the author's imagination. Any resemblance to actual people, living or dead, or to institutions, events or locales are entirely coincidental.

Illustrations by Annie Hart
Cover design by Maegan Beaumont

Printed in the United States of America
ISBN 978-1-7368387-0-9, paperback
ISBN 978-1-7368387-1-6, ebook

First Edition

Acknowledgments

I have received many helpful suggestions from Nancy Handzo, Ann Losee, and Lee Upton. Annie Hart has been patient and cooperative in the preparation of illustrations for this volume. I am most grateful to Peter Losee for guiding these stories through the publication process.

Table of Contents

A Reluctant Conspiracy 1
The Value of Commitment 4
The Parental Inquisition 6
Tick Tock 9
Max Learns a Lesson 13
A Violation of Homestead Security 15
Maude Smith-Grabowski, P. I. 20
Max's Blue Ribbon 23
A Day in the Park with Max 26
Max and Maude: Party Animals 29
Maude's Pursuit of an Epic Life 32
The Nose Knows 34
Fish a la Cart 37
Cheese 41
The Trip 44
Intervention 47
The Voyeur 50
The Exterminator 54
Freedom and its Consequences 57
Maude Smith-Grabowski, Diva 61
Max and the Bone Thief 63
Maude Forms a Clowder 65
The Saga of Sid the Squirrel 68
A-Tenting We Will Go 71
Max Loves Patty 76

Trouble at Polk Park 81

At the Beach 85

A Visit from Rose Grabowski 88

A No-Drug Zone 91

Steve, the Real Estate Developer 94

Maude Meets Her Prince 98

Mutiny at Polk Park 102

Maude Reorganizes Sleeping Arrangements 106

Up a Tree 109

Max the Diagnostician 113

Rose Leaves Frank 116

Not on Our Watch 120

The Cat on His Back Knows Naught About That 124

Maude the Oracle 128

Pet Parade 131

Dealing with Cheryl 135

Lost in Millwood 138

Why Not a Trio? 143

Sharon's Return 147

Harmony Restored 151

Kids Are Not Welcome Here 155

Onyx 158

Onyx on Probation 161

Probation Resolved 164

Onyx in Demand 168

A Cure for Boredom 170

III

Bastet Rules	173
The Perfect Dog	175
Paralysis of the Senses	178
A Visit from Ollie	182
The Baron Banished	187
Max Fingers a Drug Mule	190
Sharon Makes Some Bad Choices	194
At Home with Sharon	197
The Price of Gluttony	200
A Reality Check for Max	203
Max Gets Even	207
Black Cat Crossing	211
Hollywood Beckons	215
What Price Fame?	218

A Reluctant Conspiracy

Maude, a golden-haired Persian, had become accustomed to being in charge of the Smith-Grabowski household. Then one day Max, a brown and black shepherd-terrier-boxer mix, arrived to establish occupancy.

Maude sought to impose some house rules:

1. My food bowl is off limits, likewise my water dish.
2. All horizontal surfaces above the floor are mine.
3. No barking is permitted at any mice found on the premises. These prey are mine.
4. Barking during my morning or afternoon naps is expressly forbidden.
5. Any disturbance of my litter box will be dealt with severely.

Max was unimpressed. "For a creature whose behavior shows no respect for rules, you sure seem keen to invent and apply them. Be advised. I am a dog. Dogs do not recognize rules invented by cats." He decided that some action was required. He noted that the back door was ajar. "I just saw three mice scamper into the garage," he announced.

Maude took the bait, streaking through the open door and into the garage. Max promptly applied his nose to nudge shut the door. Maude spent unwanted hours outside until the homeowners returned.

Maude found no mice in the garage. She realized she'd been tricked by a member of a lower species. She made a mental note that this called for retribution.

The next day Maude was relaxing on her favorite window ledge. She observed a delivery man advancing. He was carrying a package. Maude notified Max of the intruder. Max began his most threatening barking routine. The delivery man, startled, dropped the package he was carrying. There was a tinkling sound as the package hit the cement step. The delivery man left a note on the package, implicating Max. The homeowners returned that afternoon, read the note, and exiled Max to the cellar.

"Two can play this game," thought Max. The next day he applied his canine teeth to the arm of a living-room chair. Maude received blame for this crime. The homeowners carried Maude to the authorized scratching post and lectured her sternly on proper scratching behavior. Maude yawned, stretched languidly and resumed her nap.

That evening there was a Smith-Grabowski conference. Present were Emily Smith and Sharon Grabowski. Emily was a petite 27-year-old beauty, with auburn hair and hazel eyes. Sharon was a year older and two inches taller. She too was attractive, with dark brown hair and eyes. Some Millwood residents took Emily and Sharon to be sisters. Those more inclined to gossip exchanged whispers about their joint tenancy.

Emily and Sharon agreed that the present menagerie was unwelcome. Sharon suggested relocation of Max and Maude to the Happy Days Animal Shelter. Emily reluctantly agreed. Unknown to them, Max overheard this plot.

The next morning, on the way to telephone the shelter, they came upon the former combatants. Peace had broken out. Max had found a patch of sunlight on the living-room rug. Maude was curled up beside him, sharing the warmth. Emily and Sharon abandoned the idea of relocation. Max said to Maude, "I saved your bacon there, Maude. You owe me."

The Value of Commitment

Max noticed a cooling of the relationship between Emily and Sharon. He alerted Maude to the situation.

Maude shrugged. "Hey, my bowl is full, my litter box is prepared regularly, and my naps are undisturbed. Why should I be bothered by the recriminations and tears of my servants at night? What counts is that they continue to serve me."

Max replied, "That's just the point. It may be that they no longer will be available to serve your needs. I heard them talking about us last night, and I did not like what I heard."

Sharon had said, "It seems that Max and Maude have bonded so strongly. It would be cruel to separate them. Besides, which one would remain with each of us?"

Emily had replied, "That is one thing you're right about. They should either both remain here with me or both leave with you."

Sharon then objected, "I beg your pardon. Both our names are on the lease. What makes you think that I'm the one to leave?"

Emily's reply was caustic. "Because it was you who broke our relationship, and with Trudy of all people."

Sharon was dismissive. "Well, your attitude toward relationships is very 'dog-like.' You require complete servitude forever."

"Better slavish dog-like devotion than the self-centered calculating attitude of the cat," Emily said.

Sharon summed up the situation. "I guess a decision is required here. You need the simple-minded devotion of Max, whereas I appreciate the free spirit of Maude. And yet it would be a shame to separate them. Unlike you and me, they seem to be in a committed relationship."

"Do you see the problem, Maude?" Max said. "It appears our future is uncertain. There are four options: 1) you and I are together with Emily; 2) you and I are together with Sharon; 3) you are alone with Emily; or, 4) you are alone with Sharon. Which of these options should we promote?"

Maude's response was congenial. "You know, for a dog you're not bad. I find that menacing bark reassuring, you respect my territory, and your body exudes a pleasant warmth. Given these virtues, I can overlook your persistent bad breath. I propose we demonstrate to our servants that we are inseparable. Perhaps we can show them the value of fidelity in a relationship."

Maude and Max vowed to be joined at the hip. Whenever Max changed his position, Maude followed, and *vice versa*. Whenever Max was taken out for a walk, Maude sat patiently by the door. Upon Max's return, Maude would leap up excitedly, rubbing against him. "This is nauseous behavior," thought Maude, "but I am beginning to see Sharon's eyes glaze over."

After several days, the atmosphere in the house turned to one of love and harmony. Unknown to Max and Maude, this change was due to Sharon's discovery that Trudy had certain undesirable character traits. Sharon approached life with Emily with renewed enthusiasm.

Of course, Maude took credit for this positive development. The downside, as she saw it, was the continuing need to exude enthusiasm over the presence of Max in the household.

The Parental Inquisition

Maude, undaunted by the old adage about curiosity, was eavesdropping on a conversation between Sharon and Emily. "Emily, we have a problem," Sharon declared. "Mom called this morning and asked if she and Dad could stay with us Friday night on their East Coast trip. What could I say? I feigned delight and invited them for dinner. They're scheduled to arrive mid-afternoon on Friday. I know this is a disaster, but I couldn't think of a plausible reason why we wouldn't be home."

Emily did her impression of the Brit with a stiff upper lip. "It's all right," she replied, "our story is that we are two professional women who share a house. Let tongues wag if they must."

Maude was confused. She pictured Max. "Surely it is tails that wag," she thought. "Emily must mean 'let tongues drool if they must.'"

"Fortunately, we have three rooms that could be used as bedrooms," Sharon continued. "We need to move your things into the guest bedroom. We then could put my parents in the room that we now use as a study."

"There is one small problem," Emily replied. "There's no bed in the study, just a pair of desks and a recliner. We could relocate one of the desks to the basement, but there still would be no place to lie down."

"OK, how about this?" Emily offered. "We move the recliner as well to the basement. We then replace it with a futon, which will double as a sofa when not expanded. Of course we need to get one delivered and set up as a bed before Friday afternoon."

Maude reported this exchange to Max. "Why all the rearrangement?" she asked Max. "Sharon and Emily could remain in the room they share, and simply make available the guest room to her parents."

"You have a point," Max replied, "but I do like the idea of adding a futon to the study. Futons are supremely comfortable places for dog naps."

Maude returned to the cohabitation issue. "Do you suppose that Sharon doesn't want her parents to know that she shares a bedroom with Emily?" she asked Max.

"I don't know why she would be ashamed of Emily," Max replied. "Emily's great. She fills our bowls regularly. And she gives me extensive responsibilities in recognition of my superior leadership ability."

"Good points, Max," Maude replied, "but the mystery remains. Why this sudden rearrangement of bedrooms?"

Sharon and Emily selected a futon at Fulton Furniture that evening. After a day of moving, the house was ready for the dreaded invasion. Max and Maude were instructed to be respectful, and preferably to be seen and not heard.

Frank and Rose Grabowski arrived as scheduled. Emily had arranged to be at her office until just before dinner. The inquisition began almost at once. "What do we tell our friends about you and Emily?" Rose demanded. "You can imagine the rumors."

Max was not sure what was going on, but he did not like Rose's accusatory tone. He decided to defuse the situation by means of a charm offensive. Nudging Rose's knee with his nose, Max extended his right paw with what he took to be an ingratiating smile. Rose ignored him. "Not now Max," admonished Sharon. "Go lie down."

Max was on his way to his bed in the kitchen when the phone rang. It was Emily, calling to say that, on the spur of the moment, she had been invited to accompany her co-worker Dennis to an off-Broadway play. Sharon conveyed the news to her parents. "Emily has a last-minute date with Dennis, a very good looking and eligible paralegal in the office."

Maude smiled. She recalled Sharon and Emily talking about Dennis and his preoccupation with spending time in his closet.

Maude approved of closets, particularly if there were gloves and hats there, upon which she could stretch out.

"Emily sends her regrets," said Sharon. "She and Dennis are going to a revival of *The Man Who Came to Dinner*. She will be home late."

"Well, good for Emily," Rose conceded. "Now how about you, Sharon?" Rose was a husky woman of whom one might expect numerous offspring. Sharon, however, was her only child. "We're counting on you to continue the Grabowski line," Rose continued. Frank grunted agreement.

Sharon remained silent. She recognized that any response would only promote further discussion of this issue.

Max's sympathies were with Sharon. "Why this concern with producing more offspring?" he asked Maude. "It seems to me that there are more than enough human beings on the planet now."

"I agree with you about that," Maude replied. "But you have to understand the biological imperative at work here. Human beings are gene-transmitting machines. They seek at all costs to ensure that their genes are present in successive generations. It is because of this 'gene-transmission imperative' that Rose is unhappy about Sharon's sexual indifference to males. Rose is afraid her genes will perish with Sharon."

"You always teach me new things about our human friends," Max replied. "I never realized how greatly they value 'hand-me-down' jeans."

Tick Tock

Max approached the very attractive standard poodle. She clearly was the most interesting dog in the park. "Hi there, gorgeous," he began. "Do you come to the park often?" The poodle remained aloof, as if Max were not there. Max decided to try a little male humor. "Normally I require a substantial stud fee," he told her. "But today is your lucky day. I am distributing freebies as a promotional venture."

This humor was lost on the poodle. "Get lost, before I notify my owner of your evil intentions," she warned. "I can't imagine she would approve of a litter whose members possess genes derived from such a multi-breed donor. So long, mutt."

It took Max a minute to process this insult. He took this initial rejection to be a challenge. He was about to show this arrogant poodle what's what when her owner arrived. The owner, a large woman with a distinctive underbite, cast a stern, disapproving look at Max.

Max chose to leave the scene. The encounter had not increased his feeling of self-worth. He returned home in a black mood.

At home, Emily's parents were in residence for a brief visit. The Smiths did not share the Grabowskis' concern about Emily's sex life. There was no inquisition on this topic. Instead, the Smiths were anxious to exhibit photos from their recent trip to Bavaria. Sharon joined Emily in a chorus of "oohs" and "ahs" as Fran Smith passed around views of "Mad King" Ludwig's castle Neuschwanstein. Her internal reaction was different. "Why go to Bavaria?" she thought. "There's a perfectly good replica at Disney World."

After the display of photos, Donald Smith announced that he and Fran had brought back a gift for the house. He retrieved a large package from the trunk of his car. Emily opened it. It contained a cuckoo clock. The clock was no battery-operated knock-off. It was a walnut and mahogany pendulum clock created by craftsmen in the Black Forest.

"It's beautiful," said Emily. "Thank you so much."

Sharon and Emily agreed upon a location in the living room. Donald made careful measurements and then anchored the clock to the wall.

What followed was a nightmare for Maude. Every hour the cuckoo emerged. It made a noise no bird would recognize. The situation was made worse by the fact that the cuckoo performed on the half-hour as well. Maude found that, after being assaulted by one cuckoo cry, she came fully awake waiting for the next. She was unable to sleep for more than twenty minutes at a time. Maude shared her frustration with Max. "Max," she said, "you know how grouchy I get when I don't get enough sleep. This clock has thoroughly disrupted my rhythms."

"I'm sorry," Max replied, "I myself have been able to ignore it. Perhaps in time you too will adjust to the dulcet tones of our resident bird."

"I'm desperate, Max," Maude declared. "We need to take action. I suggest that when Sharon and Emily return from work this afternoon, we combine to screech and bark every time the cuckoo appears." Max agreed to cooperate.

That evening Sharon and Emily relaxed before dinner with glasses of white wine and slices of mozzarella cheese drizzled with extra-virgin olive oil. The clock began to announce six o'clock. Max and Maude sprinted to a position beneath the clock. They commenced to screech and bark. At one point Maude leaped into the air and swiped at the cuckoo with her paw. The effect was comical. Maude missed the bird by at least two feet. Nevertheless Emily was impressed by Maude's display.

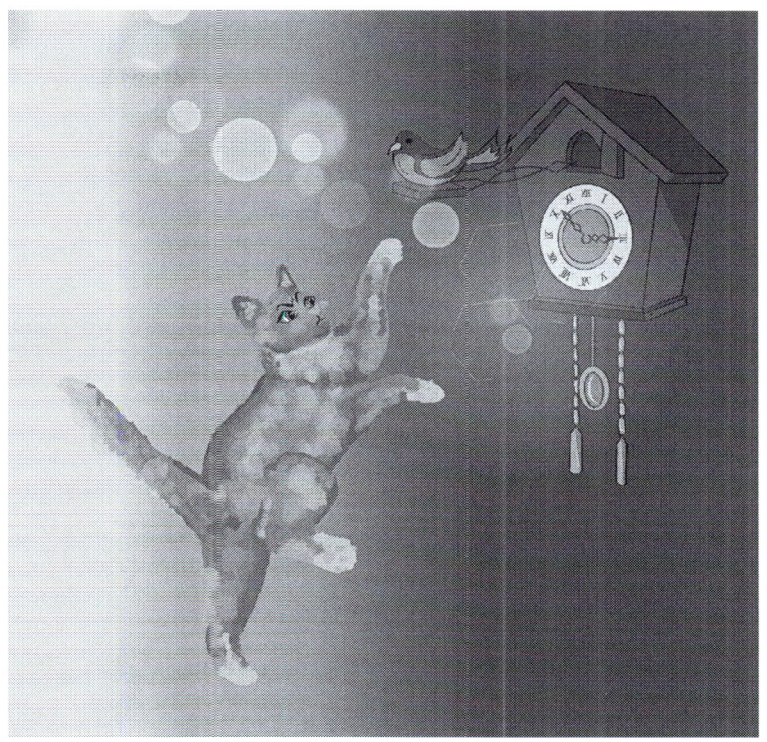

"Why are they doing this?" Sharon asked. "Do you suppose that the cuckoo noise hurts their ears?"

"I don't think so," Emily replied. "The clock is a new part of their experience. It may take a while for them to get used to it. Let's wait to see what happens."

Maude and Max took notice of their owners' reaction. Thy resolved to continue their protests upon each appearance of the cuckoo. After the eleven o'clock performance, Emily conceded. She emerged from the bedroom. Maude and Max fled into the kitchen, anticipating imminent punishment. Emily ignored them. She removed the clock from the wall in order to select the "silent operation" option on the back of the clock.

Maude slept fitfully that night, waking frequently in anticipation of a strike of the clock. The next day, however, she enjoyed both morning and afternoon naps. Maude observed that life was good again. She heaped praise on Max for his role in the "silence the cuckoo" project.

Max Learns a Lesson

Sharon and Emily were at home, enjoying a quiet evening before the TV. The doorbell rang. Max responded with an ominous bark. The visitor turned out to be neighbor Vivian, a person recognized by Max. The barking ceased, replaced by vigorous tail wagging. Vivian handed a Milk-Bone to an appreciative Max.

Vivian joined Sharon and Emily for a gin and tonic in the living room. It was obvious to Max that Vivian was upset and that she was being consoled by Sharon and Emily.

Vivian's husband Mark arrived at the door in a penitent mood. Mark appeared anxious to repair the damage caused by his explosion at Vivian's latest spending spree.

Max was fully prepared to act on behalf of his new friend Vivian. Sensing that Vivian was afraid of the intruder at the door, Max launched a volley of barks that informed the intruder that failure to beat a swift retreat would result in a need for a tetanus shot.

Mark took Max's advice and retreated to his car. Vivian, however, was impressed that Mark had made the effort to see her, presumably to apologize for his part in their quarrel. Vivian began to cry, upset that Mark had been turned away.

Max received admonishing glances. He was confused. In his subsequent exile in the cellar he tried to figure out what he had done wrong.

Maude was quick to educate him. "Max, you're a sweetheart," she began, "but perceptive you are not. From now on let me do the mental heavy lifting. I will assess the situation, consider various courses of action, and select the one that best improves the situation. This is where you come in. You will be the agent who brings about this improvement. All credit will be yours."

Mark, chased to his car by Max, phoned Sharon and Emily's house in order to talk to Vivian. Mark sought reconciliation. Hesitantly, Vivian agreed to meet Mark at his car in front of the house.

Maude had been observing carefully, and was prepared to apply her analytic prowess to the situation. It was obvious to Maude that Vivian was being led into a trap. Maude interpreted the hesitation in Vivian's voice as an indication of fear. The appropriate action obviously was to prevent Mark from kidnapping Vivian. Maude made this clear to Max, who was impressed by Maude's powers of analysis. He accepted with enthusiasm the task she assigned him.

When Mark stepped out of his car, Max lunged forward, seeking to close teeth on Mark's leg. Mark leaped to the side, and Max succeeded only in clamping down on his pant leg. This produced a ripping sound, followed by shouts of "Bad Max" from both Sharon and Emily.

Max again was exiled to the cellar. He reflected on today's life experiences. He decided that a resolution was in order. Henceforth he would ignore all future instructions from Maude.

A Violation of Homestead Security

Handyman Bert Azolina arrived at the Smith-Grabowski residence to begin construction of a small backyard patio. It was Saturday morning. Sharon was at her office, leaving Emily to oversee the construction project.

Max protested this intrusion. Bert was prepared. He produced a Milk-Bone. Max sensed that things were OK. Emily and the intruder had conversed calmly. And the intruder was in possession of treats. Max accepted the biscuit, replacing barks with wags of his tail.

Later that morning, Emily invited Bert to the kitchen for coffee. Max greeted his new friend with enthusiasm. Bert produced a liver treat. "Wow," thought Max, "that was even better than a Milk-Bone."

Max shared with Maude his high opinion of Bert. Maude was more cautious. "I know he seems to be generous," she said, "but his eyes are too close together. Human beings with narrow-set eyes are not to be trusted."

Maude's caution proved to be well-founded. As he was finishing the job Sunday afternoon, Bert discovered the emergency back door key that had been tied beneath the branch of a shrub. He returned Monday morning when Sharon and Emily were at work. He appeared to be looking for a missing tool. In the process he liberated the back door key from its hiding place.

Bert advanced to the back door. Max sensed an alien presence and commenced to bark. Bert spoke to him. "I recognize that voice," Max thought. "It's that man who brings me delicious snacks." The barking ceased, replaced with an anticipatory whine. Bert opened the door and offered Max a liver treat. Maude looked on from her windowsill perch.

Bert moved over to Max's empty food bowl, opened his carryall, removed a pre-cooked sausage patty, and dropped it into the bowl. Max was on it in a flash. Bert moved past him into the dining room. He examined closely the silver candlesticks he had noticed on

Saturday. "Excellent workmanship," he concluded, as he placed them in his carryall. He opened the drawers of the buffet. There was nothing of value there.

As he bent over to pick up the carryall, a pencil dropped from his breast pocket onto the rug. The pencil was an advertising gimmick. "Bert Azolina -- Odd Jobs" it proclaimed. Bert was unaware of this loss. Maude was not. She sauntered over and collapsed over the pencil. With the pencil under her back she presented her tummy to Bert for a rub. "Sorry Maude," he said, "I'm in a bit of a hurry."

Bert opened the front door from the inside. He then used his lock-picking tools to produce extensive scratch marks on the outside of the door lock. He hoped investigators would conclude that illegal entry to the house had been through the front door.

Bert passed through the kitchen where Max was at his water bowl after having consumed the sausage. Bert exited through the back door, locked it, and replaced the spare key in the nearby bush.

After he had gone, Maude lectured Max on homestead security. "Max," she admonished, "you are responsible for protecting Sharon, Emily and their possessions. Those candlesticks were a prized possession. They were a present from Emily's grandmother. 'English silver from the Georgian Period,' Emily had said. She loved those pieces. I might point out, in addition, that the presence of those candlesticks made the buffet the only horizontal surface I am forbidden to occupy. But that perhaps is not important. What is important is that this morning you welcomed a thief to our house. Why did you allow this? Does your stomach rule your mind?"

Emily discovered the theft upon returning home from work. She reported the incident to the Millwood Police. Sergeant Jones was dispatched to the Smith-Grabowski residence.

Max barked furiously, anxious to atone for his earlier inaction. "No, no, Max," said Maude. "Look at the uniform. This is a policeman. He captures thieves and puts them in jail."

"This homestead security responsibility is difficult for me," Max lamented. "You seem to be able to tell which human beings are a threat and which are not. I lack this ability."

"Well, you have achieved the first stage of wisdom," Maude replied. "You are aware of your own limitations. I modestly suggest that in the future you look to me for guidance in these matters."

"Maude has identified the thief," Emily told Jones. "She called attention to the pencil Bert left behind. Can't you search his place? I'll be heartbroken if grandmother's gift is lost to me forever."

Sergeant Jones' reply was not reassuring. "We can't base a request for a court order to examine Azolina's premises on the 'testimony' of a cat." Maude was outraged. She hissed in disgust as she retreated to her litter box.

Emily gave Sergeant Jones a photo of the candlesticks. Jones promised to alert area antique dealers and pawn shops to the theft.

"It's clear we're not going to get much effort from the Millwood Police," Emily said. "Is there anyone in your firm that might be able to help?"

Sharon thought for a moment. "I'll ask Sam," she said. "She knows a lot about shady internet transactions."

The next evening Sam, a petite redhead wearing glasses, arrived at the Smith-Grabowski house. She took out her laptop and gave instructions to its keyboard. On its screen an image of the candlesticks emerged. Between them was a cheap Chinese vase. The caption beneath the photo stated, "Ming Dynasty Vase — $1500". "Those are Grandmother's candlesticks," Emily declared.

"I thought so," Sam replied. "This is a website like e-Bay, but used primarily by people who want to buy and sell antiques of dubious provenance. The seller is not attempting to sell a Ming vase. Other users of the website understand this. The real objects for sale are the candlesticks. The buyer will be paying $1480 for the candlesticks and $20 for the vase."

It was agreed that Sam would use her laptop to offer to purchase the "Ming vase." The reply email specified a time and place for the exchange of goods and money. Sam was to meet the seller at noon at the furthest bench in Polk Park. She was instructed to bring a valise containing the purchase price in bills of denomination not to exceed $100.

At the time specified for the exchange, Emily sat behind sunglasses and a baseball cap in a car with a view of the bench. Max sat beside her, ready to do whatever might be required. Emily watched as a tall man—definitely not Bert—approached the bench and sat down alongside Sam. The man identified himself as "Phil." He claimed to be the authorized representative of the seller. He opened his backpack to reveal the candlesticks. Sam displayed the bills at the top of her valise.

Phil suddenly had an idea. He snatched the valise from Sam and turned to run off with it and the candlesticks. Bert would be happy to receive the cash. He would never find out that Phil had kept the candlesticks. Evidently there was no honor among thieves.

Before he could make his escape, Sam directed a stream of pepper spray at him. Unfortunately the stream was slightly off target. Phil was briefly disoriented by the spray, but managed to stagger off toward the street.

Emily left her car to give chase. Max bounded out the open door and quickly closed on the culprit. Phil turned to kick out at Max. This was a mistake. Max fastened his jaws on the outstretched ankle. Phil screamed and crashed to ground. Max stood guard as Emily retrieved both candlesticks and money. Sam called 911 on her cell phone. Phil was carried away, fully prepared to implicate Bert in the original theft.

Back home, Maude stepped out of character. She heaped praise on Max. "You were courageous when it counted. The violation of homestead security has been avenged. We are proud of you."

Max beamed. He then retreated to the kitchen to see if any treats had been added to his food bowl. Maude had expected reciprocity. "Hey Max," she cried, "you might acknowledge my role in identifying the thief."

"Quite right," he replied. "We make a good team. Between us the homestead is secure."

Maude Smith-Grabowski, P. I.

Sharon and Emily had finished setting up the four tables for the weekly duplicate bridge session. The members had selected the Smith-Grabowski house as the locale for their competition. Money spent on coffee, tea and snacks came from a $20 per person assessment. The remainder of these funds went to the winning team at the end of the competition.

The eight pairs of competitors used the same basic bidding techniques and had comparable skills in the playing of hands. And yet Liz and Francie nearly always made off with the prize money. Maude had overheard Sharon and Emily bitching about this. "Perhaps there is a job here for 'Maude Smith-Grabowski, Private Investigator,'" she mused. Maude resolved to study the Liz-Francie team at the next competition.

Max did not share Maude's interest in the game. He pretended for a time that the tossing of cards to the center of the table was a tossing of miniature pizza slices to be consumed later by himself. However, there was no olfactory aspect to the sliding of "pizzas" across the table. Max soon lost interest in the game.

Meanwhile, Maude had been studying the partnership of Liz and Francie. She noticed that Liz and Francie usually said "one heart" when announcing a bid. However, they sometimes said "I'll bid a heart." Equivalent bids, or were they? By the end of the afternoon, Maude had discovered that "one heart" was associated with a minimal bid. The occasional "I'll bid a heart," however, was associated with a stronger hand, one that fell just short of that required for an opening "two hearts" bid.

"No wonder Liz and Francie usually win the kitty," Maude remarked to Max.

Max was confused. "What are you talking about? You are the only feline in the room," he replied.

Maude snorted in disgust. "Never mind. Max. The important thing is that Liz and Francie are cheating. They are giving each other more information about their hands than the rules allow."

Max was even more confused. He failed to see what the shape of fingers or the color of nail polish had to do with the game of bridge.

"We need to alert Sharon and Emily about this," Maude said.

To avoid upsetting Maude, Max agreed,. "How do you propose to do that?"

"Let me think about it," said Maude.

By the time of the next meeting of the duplicate club, Maude had formed a plan. The first hand was played. Liz opened "one heart." Maude produced a loud "meow." Two hands later, Francie said "I'll bid a spade." Maude produced two loud "meows." Throughout the afternoon Maude coordinated the number of "meows" with the bidding terminology selected by Liz or Francie.

The numbers were crunched. Once again Liz and Francie were the winners. The players dispersed. Alone once again, Sharon posed a question to Emily. "Did you notice how intently Maude watched our game?"

"I did," Emily replied. "And she meowed only when Liz or Francie placed a bid."

"I'm glad you noticed. Did you also notice that sometimes she gave one meow and sometimes two meows? I just figured out the pattern. One meow is correlated with a weak opening bid; two meows is correlated with a strong bid that just falls short of a 'two' bid. What puzzles me is how Maude could have established the correlation. She could not see the cards in their hands at the time of the bidding."

"It must have been the way in which Liz or Francie stated the bid," Emily concluded. "Let's be on the lookout for verbal, or non-verbal, clues at our next session."

At the next session, Sharon and Emily both realized what Maude had discovered. "One heart" and "I'll bid a heart" had different meanings in the Liz-Francie universe of discourse. That evening Sharon contacted the other members of the competition. There was unanimous agreement that Liz and Francie be excluded from future meetings. Meanwhile, Maude enjoyed a dinner of sashimi-grade tuna as a reward for first-class detective work. Max sulked on his bed, at a loss to understand why Maude was receiving this special treatment.

Max's Blue Ribbon

Maude was not a fan of car rides. The rapid progression of trees and houses made her dizzy. This trip promised to be different, however. Sharon had purchased a strap-on infant carrier and Maude had been installed therein. Maude was extremely comfortable, in part because of the warmth of Sharon's body. This new arrangement made car travel tolerable. Maude elected to begin a nap.

Max was in his element. The entire back seat was his domain. He bounded from one window to the other, not wishing to miss any interesting development as the world passed by. In the front seats, Sharon and Emily compared notes on the best route to the Lynnwood Annual Dog Competition, a mere thirty miles away.

At the competition, Maude surveyed the action from her pouch on Sharon's chest. She was amazed at the stupidity of dogs. Most of the dogs present would chase her if they saw her on the ground. But secure within the infant carrier, Maude was invisible to the dogs below. She could observe their mindless behavior without fear of attack.

The dogs below took turns running, jumping over fences, navigating through tunnels, and swiveling between poles driven into the ground. Maude saw no point to this activity.

Emily, on the other hand, was trying to interest Max in the competition. Maude found this to be unrealistic. "Max," she said, "you couldn't figure out which obstacle to attack next, let alone find the finish line."

Max was appalled by Maude's lack of confidence in his ability to know what to do next. However, he had to admit that running the obstacle course was very complicated. Max preferred a direct, straightforward approach to the obstacles presented by life.

Max found a competition he liked. It was an uncomplicated, straight-line race. Dogs lined up behind a door. The door swung open. Dogs charged out in pursuit of a moving, rabbit-scented cloth doll. There were three hurdles to be cleared on the way to the finish. The dogs raced up to and over the hurdles. The first dog to pursue the cloth doll through an opening in stacked bales of hay on the finish line was the winner. Max found the simplicity of this competition appealing. It was unlike traversing an obstacle course, where you have to remember which way to turn next.

Unfortunately, the hurdle race seemed to be reserved for Jack Russell terriers. Max shared the general opinion that the Jack Russell is a yappy creature whose sanity is suspect. Max was uncertain about his ancestry, but he was certain that there were no Jack Russell terriers in the last several generations. He needed to look further for an event in which he could participate and excel.

There was a pool at the end of the property. From time to time a dog would launch himself from the edge of the pool, through the air, and into the water. The goal evidently was to land as far from the pool edge as possible. After the official competition had been completed, Max gave it a try.

Max enjoyed the sensation of flying through the air. He did not enjoy striking the water in a fully outstretched position. "Ouch," he said. "I'm not sure that life as a water-jump champion would be consistent with my preferred retirement plan—the collection of stud fees."

However, the pain soon subsided. "How did I do?" he asked Sharon.

"You jumped 16 feet, Max. And you did so with maximum style points," Sharon said while she rubbed him dry with a towel.

"All right!" said Max. "By the way, what is the record for this event?"

"The record at present is 33 feet 10 inches," Sharon commented.

"I don't believe that is possible," said Max.

"The record's held by a Belgian Malinois," Sharon continued. "They appear to be the best at this event."

Crestfallen, Max saw his dream of becoming water-jump champion vanish.

After returning home, Max was allowed to visit his buddy Prince. Prince was recovering from a bad fall. His left hind leg was in a cast. Prince's movements were constrained by a chain attached to a stake in his back yard.

As Max approached, Prince barked furiously. "This is not a welcoming bark," Max thought. Further observation revealed that it was not directed at him. There was a fox prowling around the fence that enclosed the family's chickens.

Max reacted at once. He charged the fox, announcing that he would dismember him. The fox fled the scene, with Max in hot pursuit. Well, maybe lukewarm pursuit. The fox was so much quicker. Panting freely, Max returned to a sequence of approving barks from Prince.

Prince's female owner had witnessed the chase from the kitchen window. Mrs. Andrews emerged to lavish praise on Max, eventually returning to the kitchen to fetch a rawhide bone for him.

At that point, Emily arrived and was told the story of Max's heroism. "Max," she said, "you are a real champion. Not by running around an obstacle course, but by taking action to oppose evil. Twenty chickens are grateful to you."

Emily tied a blue ribbon around Max's collar. Max wore his award proudly.

A Day in the Park with Max

Christine Pickering arrived at Polk Park with her laptop. She selected a vacant bench, mounted the laptop on her knees, and prepared to compose a story for the *Millwood Messenger* about last night's City Council meeting.

The meeting had been uneventful. The members unanimously agreed to postpone all pending decisions until the next meeting. Before reaching this point of agreement they had spent two hours posturing and insulting one another. Christine despaired of the democratic process, which seemed to feature displays of self-interest devoid of concern for the general good. She crossed her legs to bring the laptop screen closer. This didn't help. The laptop morphed into a block, thwarting the creative process. Her attention was drawn to activities in the park.

Emily had taken Max and Prince to the park. Prince was a house guest for the day while Pat Andrews put in some Saturday overtime. Prince no longer wore a cast on his leg, but he was just barely mobile.

Max took charge. He and Prince circled the park announcing that they were in command and that any misbehavior by other dogs present would be punished.

Returning to Emily's bench, Max paused to observe a mom throw a Frisbee to her six-year-old son. Mikey's return throw flew off at right angles. "I got it," said Max, executing a leap to haul it in between his jaws. Max delivered the disk to the mom. She recoiled a bit upon contact with the saliva-laden Frisbee. "Thank you, Max," she said, patting his head. Her hand was sticky but Max didn't care. He had performed a small service to promote harmony within the community of park-goers.

Mikey caught the next toss from his mother. He then launched another off-target throw. Max captured it. This time he returned the disk to Mikey. Mikey's next wild throw also was caught in the air by Max, who again dropped the Frisbee at Mikey's feet.

Mikey's mom realized that she no longer had a role in this game. Pleased with this development, she left the action to sit on the bench next to Christine.

The game proceeded for several minutes. Mikey then abandoned the Frisbee. He ran to his mother, announcing at high volume that he was ready for ice cream. Max rejoined Emily and Prince. He was panting heavily, while appearing to smile at the same time.

Emily had brought a plastic bowl and a large bottle of water in her carry-all. She placed the bowl on the ground and filled it with water. A grateful Max quickly began to rehydrate. "Ah, Vermont spring water," he thought.

Before he could find a suitable place to lie down, Max noticed a problem in the play area of the park. A young girl on the balance board was sobbing. She was stuck in the "up" position high above the ground as her heavier partner anchored the other end of the board. Max assessed the situation. He mounted the board at the lower end and walked slowly upon it toward the frightened girl. His added weight caused a gradual descent of the sobbing girl's end of the board. She quickly dismounted. Max also jumped off. The overweight partner at the other end of the board came to ground with a thump. No damage done.

The girl hugged Max as her mother reached the play area. Much praise was heaped on Max, who accepted this attention with appropriate modesty. "All is well in the park once more," he thought. But then he noticed a commotion at the far end of the park.

A distraught mother was explaining, between sobs, that she had left her three-year-old son in the care of a young girl while she left briefly to get ice cream cones. When she returned, Herbie and the volunteer minder were nowhere to be seen.

Max bounded to the scene, followed by Emily and Prince. He noticed a stuffed bear on the ground. Max absorbed its scent. "If this belongs to Herbie, there may be a trail I can follow," he thought. Max sniffed the ground, moving quickly to a space between two garbage cans and the park fence. There was Herbie, playing in the dirt with his toy truck. Max initiated his "happy barks" sequence while turning rapidly in small circles.

The distraught mother responded to Max's antics. She approached Max, who encouraged her to follow by running toward the area where Herbie was happily preoccupied. Mother and toddler were reunited. Max accepted a hug from Herbie's mother and praise from the park-goers who had witnessed his tracking prowess.

Christine Pickering had observed Max's heroics from her perch on a park bench. It was clear to her that a story about recent activity in the park would have greater reader appeal than a report of last night's council meeting. She approached Emily about this project. Emily was delighted. Christine took a photo of Max. The next day the headline under her byline read "Canine Heroism in Polk Park."

Max and Maude: Party Animals

Partygoers filled the Smith-Grabowski residence. Most were young women, holding wine glasses containing various levels of fluid. There were a few men present as well. Max was omnipresent, quite the party animal. He loved the aromas of yet-to-be-tasted cocktail snacks. Max had found that proffered "paw-shakes" were almost always accepted, and that the recipient often responded by offering him a snack. Max's tail wagged furiously as he made the rounds of the guests, introducing himself with enthusiasm.

"That's enough, Max," Sharon said sharply. "Go lie down." Max retreated to his bed in the kitchen, resolving to return to the fray after Sharon disappeared from view.

Meanwhile a group had formed around Emily at the piano. She was playing "Aura Lee" very slowly. This Civil War song had been hijacked by Elvis and turned into "Love Me Tender." The group was seeking (and failing) to impose four-part harmony on the song. Maude had a keen sense of hearing and that sense was outraged. She was convinced that she had been gifted with perfect pitch.

"That's B-natural you idiot, not B-flat," she complained. "Here—let me show you," Maude said, producing what the other singers took to be an eerie screech. Maude took the collective recoil of the group to be testimony to the beauty of her singing.

Emily quickly disabused her of this notion. Maude was removed from the scene of her crime by the scuff of her neck and deposited in the cellar.

The cellar had been spruced up a bit. Four players surrounded a newly-installed foosball game. Max sat off to the side, attracted by the sound of paddles striking the ping-pong ball. A furious exchange resulted in the ejection of the ball from the table. "I got this," Max announced, pouncing on the rolling ball. Max was proud of his retrieving skills. He gently closed his teeth on the ball. Not gently enough, alas. The celluloid cracked, leaving a bad taste in Max's mouth. The game was over, lacking a replacement ball. The players left the cellar. Max sought to follow them, but was blocked by Sharon. "You stay here with Maude," she said. "You've caused enough trouble already."

Maude and Max, alone now in the cellar, were quite depressed. All the action now was upstairs and they were trapped below. "How do we get back upstairs where the food is?" Max asked.

"I have a very simple plan," Maude replied. "Can you act as if you had an urgent need to relieve yourself? Sharon or Emily will allow you to exit the house. Perhaps when you bark for reentry, they will allow you to stay upstairs. Meanwhile I will try to sneak upstairs when someone comes to let you outdoors."

Maude's plan worked. Max and Maude were back upstairs. They approached the revelers cautiously, remaining on the periphery. Maude had suggested that they adopt a forlorn, neglected look. Thus far it was not working. The guests were so self-absorbed that they failed to notice the loveable household pets.

Lacking Maude's patience, Max elected a more direct approach. He noticed that a blond lady was trying to hold both a wine glass and a small plate containing a "pig in a blanket" in her left hand while she gesticulated with her right. Max delivered two thumps of his tail on her bare legs, producing the desired effect. The plate tipped and Max caught the "pig in a blanket" before it could hit the floor. It was delicious.

Max expected praise for his quick reflexes. What he received from Emily however, was a directive to return to his bed in the kitchen. Max was puzzled, not for the first time at this party.

The party ended with Maude purring in response to constant stroking from numerous female admirers. Max, by contrast, was restricted to his bed. It seemed to him that life was unfair. Every time he began to enjoy himself at the party someone yelled at him. Maude was much better at ingratiating herself.

"Maude," Max demanded, "How come you're always accepted and pampered by visitors to our house?"

"Well, how can I put this? Some of us have charm and others do not. It might help if you developed some *panache*."

"Is there an exercise program for that?" Max asked. "I'm good at exercising."

"I'm afraid not," Maude said. "But I can show you. You just need to follow my every instruction for the next month. *Panache* then will be yours."

Maude's Pursuit of an Epic Life

Maude was bored. Life in the Smith-Grabowski household had become altogether too predictable. Maude's rodent-extermination program had achieved complete success, thus there was no night action, nothing left to chase. Days were no better. The birds had flown off to warmer climes, thus depriving Maude of indoor window watching and outdoor stalking. One could not sleep all the time. Something had to be done.

Max was no help. His interests were strange—collecting messages from other dogs at various trees, and retrieving thrown balls and sticks. Really, he was too easily amused. But perhaps he could play a role in the drama she was planning.

Emily was in the kitchen preparing *coq au vin*. The *coq* was simmering. Emily poured some *vin* into her one-pint measuring cup. Her preparations were interrupted at this point by a call from Sharon. Sharon was in need of some wardrobe advice.

Maude appraised the situation. On the counter was wine in a measuring cup and Kibbles 'n Bits (with gravy) in Max's bowl. Maude leaped to the counter top, nudged the measuring cup over to the bowl, and tipped the cup so that a stream of wine flowed into the bowl. Lifting the cup with both paws, Maude drained its contents onto Max's evening meal. She then alerted Max to the fact that dinner was ready.

Max charged into the kitchen. He observed to his dismay that his bowl was still on the kitchen counter. His reaction to this unfortunate situation was to deliver his "pleading bark" sequence. Emily returned, responded to Max's request, and placed the bowl on Max's dining pad.

Emily redirected her attention to the *coq au vin* project. She was puzzled. There was no *vin* visible in the measuring cup. But she could not remember spiking the *coq*. She lifted the measuring cup for an aroma test. Clearly it recently had contained *vin*. "I must have added the wine before leaving to solve Sharon's problem," she concluded.

Maude had observed that *vin* drinkers fall into one of two categories—happy drunks and angry drunks. Max apparently was a happy drunk. He rubbed his body against Sharon's legs during dinner, emitting a *sotto voce* continuous bark that resembled Maude's purring activity. After the meal he established a beachhead by placing a paw on Emily's leg as she half-reclined on the sofa. This was followed by a full-bodied assault. Its result was that Max was completely sprawled over Emily's lap. Snoring sounds emerged, followed by a most impressive display of flatulence. Max was exiled to the cellar to sleep it off.

Maude rolled on the floor in uncontrolled mirth. "My life may not be epic," she said, "but it has its moments."

The Nose Knows

Emily's brother Steve arrived for dinner. Steve and Emily each received income from trust funds established by Grandfather Smith. Steve, unlike Emily, did not supplement this income by gainful employment. Instead, he was conducting research for a novel about a middle-class family trapped in a business environment dominated by automation and globalization.

Max liked Steve. Steve included him in a variety of activities—Frisbee-toss, hide-and-seek, and tennis ball keep-away with Emily or Sharon. At the conclusion of these enjoyable activities, Steve always produced a treat for Max.

Steve also had created a game for Maude. He attached one end of a cord to a hook on the basement ceiling. On the other end he attached a Nerf ball, soft but nearly indestructible. Steve set the ball in motion. Maude followed its path and swiped at it with her paw. Maude liked the game best when Steve released the ball for her. She soon found, however, that she could play the game by herself. Each swat of the ball produced a new trajectory.

"Playing with prey is fun," she thought. "But now it is time for the *coup de grace*. Timing the swing of the ball perfectly, Maude leaped and closed both paws around the ball. She returned to ground with the ball firmly imprisoned between her paws. The ball had been separated from its cord. "No, no, Maude," admonished Steve, "swatting is good, grabbing is not good. It ruins the game."

Maude refused to acknowledge rules as a matter of principle. She swatted the ball across the floor, pursued it, and swatted it again. She had flashbacks of mice pursued. Steve left her to this pursuit. "So much for creating a game to be played," he mused. "Cats will be cats."

After dinner, Steve retreated to the guest bedroom. He removed the picture section from the wallet in the breast pocket of his jacket. He returned to the living room to show Emily and Sharon pictures of his latest girlfriend. Emily complimented his taste and then remarked on the "new leather" aroma of the picture holder. "I see that you have a new wallet," she said.

Max too showed an interest in the picture holder. "Wow, that's a potent aroma," he thought.

Steve sought to restore the picture holder to his wallet. His back pocket was empty, however. "Aha," he realized, "I left the wallet in my jacket on the bed in the guest bedroom. Let's see if Max can find it." Steve waved the picture holder beneath Max's nose. He then walked over to the open bedroom door motioning for Max to follow. "Find the wallet, Max," he commanded.

Max was puzzled. What did Steve want him to do? Steve was gesturing with his hands toward the guest bedroom. Max decided to investigate. He entered the room and noticed that the new-leather aroma, which had been decreasing, now began to increase strongly. He followed the aroma to its source, nudged Steve's jacket with his nose and barked twice. "This is like hide-and-seek," Max thought. "I'm good at that game."

"Great job, Max," Steve exclaimed, "have a Milk-Bone." Max barked softly to show appreciation for the treat.

Steve decided to see if Max could track down the sources of other aromas. He cut a garlic clove in half. He hid one half in the Emily-Sharon bedroom. He then called Max into the kitchen, exposed him to the other half, and commanded Max to find its mate. Max thought, "This is easy." He followed the garlic aroma directly to its source and again barked twice.

"Well done, Max," said Steve.

Steve realized he might have a valuable resource in the dog. Could Max locate hidden packets of cocaine? Steve just happened to have a small sample hidden in his car. He acquainted Max with its distinctive aroma. He asked Emily to keep Max outside while he hid the cocaine packet behind the water heater in the basement. When Emily and Max reentered the house, Steve asked Max to locate the source of this new aroma.

Max immediately recognized the presence of this irritating aroma in the house. It appeared to originate in the basement. Max charged down the stairs, ran to the water heater, and barked twice. He had passed the decisive test. Steve presented him with a liver treat.

The next day Steve made an appointment for Max with Homeland Security at the local airport. Max was on his best behavior. He sat patiently before a baggage carousel while Steve and a security person exchanged small talk. "What's his name?" Steve was asked. "Max," Steve replied.

Pieces of luggage arrived on the carousel. Max barked twice at the fourth, seventh, tenth, fifteenth and nineteenth pieces. He scored a perfect five out of five on this test. Subsequently he proved proficient at identifying cocaine in the presence of coffee, garlic, and other disguises.

The security person prepared a contract for Max's services. Max would work as a "sniffer dog, grade 3", each Saturday and Sunday. In return, Max would receive meals and a stipend for his services. Emily and Sharon agreed that Steve should receive the stipend, on the condition that he pick up and return Max on his sniffing days.

Max enjoyed his weekend duties. He added "Homeland Security" to "household security" on his resumé. His handlers gave him much praise and rewarded him frequently with treats. The work required was easy. Max wondered why his human handlers didn't do the sniffing themselves.

At home during the week, Max's stride was confident and purposeful. At the park, he claimed, and was granted, alpha-status within the canine population. To top it off, Maude had become newly respectful.

Fish a la Cart

Maude's favorite place in the world was Fletcher's Fish Market. Emily had parked in front of Fletcher's one day last week. Maude had spent ten minutes staring through the car window at Fletcher's display windows. Behind those windows were trays of glistening, freshly caught fish, tastefully displayed on slivers of ice. The car window was open an inch at the top. Maude could smell, and almost taste, the delicacies on display.

Maude was unaware that local residents were up in arms about the delivery area behind the market. They did not share Maude's love of fish aromas. These aromas arose from a dumpster containing fish heads, fish tails, and fish carcasses that had exceeded their sell-by date.

Even though a tarpaulin was supplied with the dumpster, it was not quite long enough to provide complete coverage. Moreover, workers at the market often failed to replace it after folding it over to dump unwanted produce. Area residents called attention to this situation. In response to escalating complaints, Fletcher's replaced the dumpster with two shiny new garbage carts. Each cart had a spring-loaded cover. The cover could be opened to a stable horizontal position to facilitate dumping. In its closed position, the lid prevented animals from entering and fish aromas from leaving. Every morning a Smithers Sanitation truck arrived. The truck was equipped with lifting arms that raised and emptied the contents of each cart into the truck.

Also unknown to Maude, the delivery area was policed by a large feral tomcat who referred to himself as "The Baron." The Baron ruled by force. Every cat who entered his domain without prior permission was driven away. The Baron had long sharp claws that he deployed frequently to keep away potential rivals.

Maude had frequent daydreams about Fletcher's Market. She desperately wanted to return there. She knew that after breakfast Max was given access to the fenced-in backyard. One day she followed him out the back door. Sharon realized that this was unusual, but concluded that Maude may have sensed the presence of a mouse or chipmunk in the yard. Max soon barked for reentry. Sharon saw that Maude was sunning herself on the grass. She decided to leave Maude outside as she headed to the office.

Maude found a small opening beneath the fence. She headed for the fish market. She entered the delivery area behind the market. The Baron hissed at her.

Maude's previous encounters with her fellow cats had been amiable. She greeted The Baron cordially. "You have a great location here," she began. "Has the morning delivery been made?"

"That's not something for you to worry about," The Baron snarled. "You have five seconds to leave the area. The next time I look up you had better not be in my field of view."

"Hey," Maude replied, "We're both cats, right? We have a lot in common—in particular a love of fresh fish."

The fur on The Baron's back would have risen to form an impressive display, had it not been so matted. He attacked Maude viciously, inflicting deep wounds with his sharp claws. Maude was saved by the arrival of a market worker with a pail of fish heads. The Baron enjoyed assaulting small, well-groomed cats who strayed into his territory, but he enjoyed fresh fish heads even more. Maude took advantage of The Baron's gluttony. She limped off toward home.

Maude reached home and collapsed on the grass by the front door. Shortly thereafter, next-door neighbor Sandy Kerr spotted her from her living room window. Maude was in obvious distress. Sandy approached Maude, picked her up, and placed her in the front seat of her car. Sandy drove to a nearby animal hospital and carried Maude inside. A vet on duty determined that no bones were broken, dressed Maude's wounds, and gave her a sedative.

Sharon returned home immediately after Sandy called. "Sandy," I can't thank you enough. You are a genuine Good Samaritan. I'm sure Maude will want to thank you when she wakes up," Sharon said.

Maude slept fitfully. The Baron invaded her dreams. Awake at last, Maude related the details of her misadventure to Max. "That bastard," Max said, "I'll teach that tomcat a lesson."

The next morning Emily took Max to the park. When she encountered a friend she had not seen for some time, Max took advantage of the distraction. He ran quickly to Fletcher's Fish Market. Max peered around the corner of the building to the delivery area behind. He spied The Baron, who was perched on top of an open garbage cart. The Baron was peering down at the fish remains in the cart below.

Moving stealthily, Max advanced to a position beneath the open lid. He barked loudly. The Baron, startled, fell into the cart. "Now you're in for it," Max thought, as he jumped up, striking the underside of the lid with his nose. The cart cover moved up. Its spring engaged. The lid clamped shut. The Baron, scrambling desperately, was submerged in assorted fish remains.

The Baron's first thought was "this is heaven." His second thought was that he had a problem. He could not scale the inner wall of the cart. And even if he could, he had no way to force open the lid. The Baron realized that he was trapped inside the cart.

The Baron was in luck. A truck from Smithers Sanitation arrived. The Baron felt himself lifted into the air and dropped into the interior of the truck. He scrambled up and over the side before the compacting process began.

Unfortunately, The Baron did not have time to select a landing spot in advance. He landed on his paws, as cats do. However, his front paws made contact with the sloping sides of an overturned wheelbarrow. Both front legs were severely sprained. For the next several weeks, The Baron was almost completely immobile. The local feline population strayed at will through the delivery area. The Baron could only hiss at the intruders.

Cheese

Max and Maude were in firm agreement about the excellence of cheese. Early Saturday morning Emily took Max on a shopping trip to the Cheshire Cheese Shoppe. Max's role was to guard the car while Emily was inside. Max took this responsibility seriously. His growls surprised and annoyed several passersby.

Emily returned with two bags filled with assorted cheeses—cheddar and stilton from England, brie and Camembert from France, mozzarella from Italy, Gouda from the Netherlands, and manchego from Spain. A third bag contained selected crackers.

Max initially was allowed to sit on the back seat next to the bags. However, while stopped at a traffic signal, Emily noticed that Max was producing a continuous drool that threatened the integrity of the contents of the bags. Max was directed to occupy the front passenger seat where Emily could keep an eye on him.

The shopping expedition was in service of a wine and cheese party to be held that evening. In advance of the festivities, Sharon was cutting a piece of cheddar into bite-sized cubes. Her knife cut through the hard cheese, sending a cube flying off the edge of the table. Max had been sitting patiently at the end of the table. On the appearance of the cheddar cube, he launched himself into the air, mouth open to surround it. He had miscalculated its trajectory, however. Landing on all four paws, he quickly turned to relocate the cheese. There on the floor, licking her whiskers, was Maude. "That was a two-year old cheddar, I believe," she said, smiling at Max.

Max growled to indicate his displeasure at this turn of events. Sharon defused the situation by feeding Max a newly prepared cheddar cube. The two animals professed satisfaction with this resolution.

Emily was not a fan of cocktail parties. She avoided them whenever possible. Ordinarily she would not have entertained the idea of hosting one. In this instance, however, she had an ulterior motive. The Chief Paralegal for Klinghofer, Cohen, Esposito and

Smart had announced her retirement. Emily was hopeful that she would be selected to replace her. The firm had a policy of promoting from within.

Emily found the Chief Paralegal position highly desirable. The salary was much higher than her present salary. The Chief Paralegal distributed the workload among members of the paralegal staff. As Chief, Emily could devote her attention to settling estates and formulating pre-nuptial agreements. She could delegate to underlings deed searches and the preparation of power-of-attorney forms. In addition, the Chief Paralegal was a *de facto* member of search committees for new members. The Chief also had input on salary decisions for members of the paralegal staff. Hence the wine and cheese party in honor of retiring Chief, Miriam Winters.

Emily had researched wine-and-cheese pairings. She had placed a card listing recommended cheeses around the neck of each wine bottle. "If this doesn't impress the male attorneys of the firm, I don't know what would," she said to herself.

The answer was Karen Zweig in an expensive black dress with a plunging neckline. Karen also had her eyes on the Chief Paralegal position. In the past, Emily and Karen had worked well together. Their relationship was based on mutual respect. Neither one regarded the other as a rival in the sphere of sexual relations. The vacancy in the Chief Paralegal position changed the dynamic of their relationship.

Karen was hard at work during the party. Her routine featured a melodious laugh and a subtle arm-stroking whenever her partner of the moment made what he believed to be a clever observation.

Max called Maude aside for a conference. "I thought that a gold band on the fourth finger of the left hand meant that you were 'off limits,'" he said. "The gold band functions like the red shirt worn by quarterbacks during practice." "That's a good comparison, Max," Maude replied. "It turns out that some women do not respect the 'red shirt.'"

Maude applied her considerable analytical powers to the situation developing at the party. Emily and Karen clearly were rivals. Both were intelligent and attractive, but Karen had a decisive advantage. The prey in their hunt all were men. Karen seized the opportunity to play seductress. Emily regarded such strategy as both unprofessional and distasteful. Unfortunately, it was clear that Karen was winning the contest. Maude outlined a plan to Max.

Maude and Max waited until Karen had filled her glass with red wine. Karen held her glass at face level. She did so to call attention to her "hot burgundy" lipstick. Karen's lips glowed with an intensity that the Rioja in her glass could not match.

Maude approached. She brushed her tail across Karen's ankle and smiled up at her. Karen smiled back, relieved to see that the contact was initiated by a friendly housecat and not a rodent of some sort. Max then applied his wet, rough tongue to the back of Karen's left calf. This had the desired effect. Red wine sloshed over the rim of Karen's glass, producing a deep red stain from her neck downward.

Max left the scene of his crime in the resulting confusion. His expression said, "I don't know how that could have happened."

Jason Smart, one of the firm's partners, immediately applied his handkerchief to the area of wine-stained flesh. Karen recoiled and smiled demurely as Smart withdrew his handkerchief in obvious embarrassment.

Sharon provided a robe for Karen to wear as the Rioja-soaked dress received treatment in the laundry room. Karen-the-victim was the center of attention for the duration of the party.

The following Monday, the partners selected Karen Zweig to be Chief Paralegal. Upon hearing the news, Maude concluded ruefully that the best intended, best executed, plans may have unforeseen and unintended consequences.

The Trip

Max and Maude climbed the stairs to the second floor. The Sharon-Emily bedroom door was ajar as they had hoped. Max nudged it open and they took possession of the room. Maude leaped up on the windowsill. She enjoyed watching the activity below. Max sighed contentedly as he stretched out on the bed. He found this to be an ideal spot for a nap.

Maude noticed two half-filled suitcases on the floor. She decided to test Max's powers of reasoning. "Max," she asked, pointing to the suitcases with her paw, "what does this mean?"

Max peered over the edge of the bed. "I suppose that Sharon and Emily have bought so many clothes that there is no space left in the bureau. The cases are there to store the overflow."

"They do have a lot of clothes," Maude said. "You are right about that. Do you notice anything else?"

"Well," Max suggested, "there are two pairs of shoes in Sharon's case and only one pair in Emily's."

"That's very observant. But you have overlooked something essential. Notice the wheels and handle on each case. I believe that the clothes inside are to be worn on a trip away from home."

"I hope you are wrong, Maude. There are clothes there for several days. This is an alarming development. Who will feed us while they are gone?"

The answer to Max's question was Emily's young niece, Susan. Susan made a good initial impression. She presented treats for both Max and Maude. The next morning Susan returned to take charge as Sharon and Emily left to begin a week-long cruise. Max was delighted when Susan reached for his leash. He walked obediently beside her as they headed to Polk Park. Susan shared a park bench with a friend, allowing Max to assert his authority over the other dogs in the park.

Upon return to home base, Max informed Maude that this week with Susan was going to be great. Dinner featured fresh tuna for

Maude and ground beef for Max. Maude accepted the plate of tuna graciously. After all, it was appropriate to her status as Queen of the household, even though it was not sashimi grade. Max was enthusiastic about his ground beef. He showed his appreciation by rubbing against Susan's legs while emitting his imitation-purr growl.

At this point the doorbell rang. Max advanced to a guard position before the front door. He had barked twice to alert Susan. Susan opened the door. She welcomed the intruder with a kiss. Max had seen similar behavior before. He relaxed as Susan introduced Rick. Max endured the inevitable petting of his head.

Susan and Rick assumed positions on the sofa. After a period of amiable conversation, Rick closed the distance between them. More kissing followed. The two bodies collapsed into a horizontal position on the sofa. Susan nearly disappeared from view. Max heard a muffled cry of "wait." He took that to be a cry for help. As head of household security he was obligated to respond. An extra-loud bark gained Rick's attention. He turned his head around only to see Max in mid-flight. Max landed on Rick's back, prepared to protect his new friend Susan. "No, no," Susan screamed, "Rick is a friend." Max emitted a low growl and dismounted. He kept a watchful eye on Rick, however.

Rick was shaken by this encounter with Max. He quickly departed the scene. Susan was not pleased. "I suppose you mean well, Max, "she said, "but you have just ruined a budding relationship. To the basement with you," she directed.

Maude arrived to console Max. "It was an honest mistake. You meant well. Unfortunately you are not very perceptive about the behavior of our human friends."

"What did I miss?" Max asked. "Well," Maude began, "you need to understand human mating practices. To do so, you need to put aside what you know about the behavior of dogs. With you canines there is no subtlety, no courtship. You remember your encounter with that Shih Tzu in the park?"

Max did recall the incident. If dogs could blush, he would have been blushing. "I don't understand," he complained, "what did I do wrong?"

"Not a thing, Max, forget it," said Maude.

Maude's lecture was interrupted by a scream from the kitchen. "Eek, a mouse!" exclaimed Susan.

Max did what he always did when he didn't know what to do. He began to bark. "Stand back," Maude demanded, "this is a job for a cat." She bounded up the stairs. Maude trapped the mouse in a corner of the kitchen. "I wonder how it got onto the house?" she asked herself as she neutralized this threat to household security.

Max arrived to congratulate Maude for a job well done. He noticed, however, that Susan's face had gone pale. "Maude," he said, "I don't think Susan is happy to see you batting a dead mouse around on the kitchen floor."

Maude stopped in mid-swat. She looked at Susan. "You're right," she said, "I see that she is upset. What I take to be great fun, she finds nauseating. You have taught me something I didn't know about our human friends. Imagine that. Our roles have been temporarily reversed."

Intervention

Steve opened his laptop. He assumed a thoughtful expression. Nothing came to him. He reached for the vodka martini. A few sips might get the creative juices flowing. Still nothing. He studied the passing travelers from his vantage point in the airport bar. Such ordinary, uninteresting people. Perhaps that was the point. After all, his novel was to be about the dislocation of people by automation and globalization. He sighed, noticed that his glass was empty, and ordered another.

Steve had driven Max to the airport for drug-sniffing duty. Max always received a warm welcome from the staff. Max, in turn, was proud of the respect shown him by his handlers. The occasional snacks were an added treat. He looked forward to each weekend at the airport.

This day had been uneventful. Max had found nothing suspicious in the parade of items on the luggage carousel. There was action on the ride home, however. Steve had consumed one or two vodka martinis in excess of what was prudent. His driving was, to put it charitably, erratic. A patrolman noticed a discrepancy between the rectilinear roadbed and the zigzag path of Steve's vehicle. Steve was invited to demonstrate to Officer Benson that he could place one foot in front of the other so as to describe a straight line. Steve wobbled a bit. Benson then administered a Breathalyzer test. The result was on the far side of sobriety.

Officer Benson took the wheel of Steve's car and drove them to the Millwood Police Station. Steve was charged with driving while intoxicated. A phone call brought Emily and Sharon to the station. Sister Emily apologized for Steve's lapse. She drove Steve back to the Smith-Grabowski residence. Sharon had arrived back home before them.

Max bounded from the car to the front door. He was first to enter when the door opened. "Aha,'" he exclaimed, observing the people assembled inside, "a party. I like parties."

The guests all were friends of Steve. Max zeroed in on Alan, who on prior occasions had been a reliable source of snacks. He approached Alan, tail wagging furiously. The ensuing paw-shake was followed by head-petting but no snack. Max paused to absorb the aromas in the room. He registered various perfumes, deodorants, and missed opportunities to apply a deodorant. But no food aromas. The coffee aroma emanating from the kitchen was not an acceptable substitute. "This is not good," Max thought, "I had hoped for some snacks before dinner."

"Why are all these people here?" he asked himself. He posed the question to Maude, who had descended from the lap of Emily's co-worker Grace.

"This is not a party," Maude explained. "These people are here to confront Steve about his drinking problem. Our human friends refer to this as an 'intervention.'"

Emily was the acknowledged leader of the intervention. "Steve," she began. Unfortunately, the object of the intervention had passed out on the sofa. It was clear that a lecture, however eloquent, would not be fruitful.

Sharon provided coffee for those who desired a caffeine boost. Steve, who needed this the most, was incapable of accepting a cup. The members of the intervention party soon dispersed to the winds, leaving Emily and Sharon to confront Steve in the morning.

Emily and Sharon planned to get Steve to admit that he had a problem and then insist that he enroll in the Alcoholics Anonymous program. Before they could begin, Steve provided his own analysis of the situation. It seems that he was the victim of circumstances. In the first place there was Jennifer. Their dates always involved the consumption of alcohol. Jennifer was an enabler. In the second place, the weekend airport visits placed him in an environment of bars. Since he currently was at an impasse in his "Great American Novel" project, he entered these Temples of Bacchus in order to recover the creative energy needed for his work. This too was an enabling environment."

"Today I am at a crossroad," Steve announced. "I shall jettison Jennifer. This will remove one enabling situation that leads to alcohol consumption. I also shall not stay at the airport after delivering Max for drug-identification duty. From now on I am Steve Smith, a model of sobriety."

Max and Maude witnessed this performance. "Good for Steve," Max said to Maude.

"I'm not convinced," Maude replied. "I heard Emily tell Sharon that Jennifer had dumped him. And Steve certainly will not be driving you to the airport on weekends. His driving license was suspended. So his pledge to avoid 'enabling situations' comes to nothing. Alcoholics are full of excuses for their state. Steve needs to acknowledge that he himself is the problem, not external circumstances. I'm sure Emily recognizes this."

"But he seems so sincere," Max insisted. "I think he should be given time to reform."

Emily was having none of it. "Steve," she said firmly, "your friends were here last night to demand that you acknowledge your addiction. You must admit to yourself that you simply cannot consume one drink and then stop. One drink leads to another, and another, and then another, until . . . . You must shun alcohol entirely. Alcoholics Anonymous has a program to provide support as you begin the journey toward sobriety. We want you to attend tonight's AA meeting and learn about its program."

Emily paused to see whether Steve was on board. In response, Steve spoke highly of the AA program. "I have a friend who has been in the program for several years," he reported. "Bert claims it has turned his life around. I guess it wouldn't hurt to give it a try."

"Good," Emily said, "I'll pick you up at 7:45. The meeting is at 8 o'clock."

Maude's appraisal of the situation was dark. "He won't be home when you arrive," she muttered under her breath.

The Voyeur

Emily and Sharon liked their mornings to begin as Nature intended, with the sky becoming light under the first rays of the sun. To experience this they left up the bedroom window shade 24 hours a day.

One evening, after donning sleepwear and turning off the lights, Sharon glanced out the bedroom window. She thought she saw a person running from the backyard. She told Emily about this. "Do you suppose we have attracted a *voyeur*?" she asked. "We have been rather careless about undressing in front of the window."

Max sought to make sense of this conversation. "What is a *voyeur*?" he asked Maude.

"A *voyeur* is a sort of spy," Maude said. "But the *voyeur*, unlike the spy, is not collecting information. He is observing because it gives him pleasure to observe."

"That is a strange was to get pleasure," Max responded. "But assuming that that there are such people, I see a money-making opportunity here. Perhaps we could persuade Emily and Sharon to issue tickets for each evening's performance. We could enjoy tuna and ground beef every day."

"Max, your insensitivity to the situation is appalling. Emily and Sharon are very upset that they might be watched in this way. We need to find a way to help them. I have it," she declared after a few moments' thought. She jumped up to the shelf in the open bedroom closet. Issuing a series of "meows," she persistently pawed the camera case on the shelf.

"Why is Maude pawing the old film camera?" Emily asked. "We haven't used it in years. The cameras in our cell phones are just as good, and we get to see the results right away."

"Maude is smart," Sharon observed. "There must be some reason for her calling attention to our old camera. Perhaps she does not associate picture-taking with our cell phones. . . . Wait a minute. The film camera can do something that our phones cannot. If we were to load it with infrared-sensitive film, we could record images in the dark. If the *voyeur* comes back, we could catch him in the act on film."

"Maude has a good plan," Emily said. "I'll buy a roll of infrared film tomorrow. If the intruder returns, we'll get proof of his presence.

The next night Emily was on strip-tease duty in the lighted bedroom. Sharon was in the darkened kitchen below, camera at the ready. Sharon could make out the outline of a figure standing on the bench in front of the arborvitae that enclosed the backyard. She took several shots of this apparition.

Max was absorbed within a dream. He was about to exact suitable revenge on the standard poodle who had insulted him at the park. Sharon insisted that he awaken. "This is not proper routine," Max thought. "I was outside in the backyard earlier tonight. It is now time for sleeping."

Max was a bit groggy as Sharon attached his leash. Then, in a further departure from routine, she led him out the front door. Sharon indicated that he was to go around the house into the backyard.

"Doesn't she know that the kitchen door leads directly into the backyard?" he wondered. "Of course she does," he answered his own question. "There must be some reason she let me out the front door instead. Perhaps it is a matter of household security." Max's alertness level increased on realization of this possibility. He remembered the earlier discussion about a *voyeur* in the backyard. "That must be it," he said to himself, "I remember that Sharon and Emily had been talking about an intruder."

Max charged around the house. He heard a "thump" followed by a cry of pain from the area in front of the arborvitae that provided privacy from passersby on the sidewalk beyond.

The thump and cry of pain were the products of the *voyeur's* hasty dismount from his perch on the bench that faced the bedroom window. He limped off onto the sidewalk behind the house. Max closed quickly on this threat to household security. After two warning barks he prepared to capture a leg of the enemy. Max failed to complete this project. The *voyeur* directed at Max the contents of a can of pepper spray. Max howled in pain, temporarily unable to see. Sharon rescued him. She led him back to the kitchen, where she administered wet towels to his face. Sharon and Emily lauded Max as a champion of household security. They awarded him a Milk-Bone for valor in combat, and allowed him to resume his dreams on his bed.

On the day that the developed film was delivered, the family gathered in the living room for after-dinner cognac, rawhide, and "Temptations (salmon flavor)." "I recognize that man," Emily said. "He is John Stiles, a teacher at Millwood Elementary. Sixth grade, I think. This is awkward. He has a good reputation at the school. Should we report him, to the police?"

Max adopted the posture of a judge pronouncing sentence. He recalled the pepper-spray incident. "No punishment is too harsh for this pervert," he declared.

Maude took a more lenient approach. She had not been exposed to pepper spray. "Of course *voyeurism* should be condemned," she conceded. "But *voyeurs* seldom, if ever, commit crimes of sexual abuse. I think Mr. Stiles should be required to enroll in a course that teaches respect for privacy. Perhaps some community service at a women's shelter also would be appropriate."

"Maude, you're not living in the real world," Max muttered.

Sharon and Emily had the responsibility of deciding John Stiles' fate. Sharon supported Max's position. "No person guilty of *voyeurism* should be allowed to teach our children," she maintained. "We need to report him to the police."

Emily disagreed. She pointed out that Stiles was well-regarded at Millwood Elementary and that he was active in various organizations that benefited the community. She emphasized that reporting him to the police would ruin his career and deprive the town of an important asset.

It had become clear that agreement could not be reached at this time. Emily and Sharon postponed until the following day their decision on John Stiles' future. Emily then unwrapped the translucent shade she had purchased on the way home from work. When installed, the shade allowed passage of considerable light from the early morning rays of the sun. The shade also was opaque, guaranteeing privacy (provided that one of the bedroom's occupants remembered to lower it).

.

The Exterminator

"There is a mousetrap in the corner of the kitchen," Maude exclaimed. "A mousetrap! I never have been so insulted in my life! What do you know about this, Max?"

"Well, I heard Sharon complain yesterday about a string of crumbs on the kitchen counter," Max replied. "But I don't know what that has to do with mice."

Maude clearly was angry. "I take this to be a repudiation of my rodent-management program," she said at full volume. "I need to reestablish my credentials as 'The Exterminator.'"

That evening Maude was alongside Max when Emily let him out into the backyard. Maude headed for the neighbor's garage. There was no space for cars there. The Blodgetts used the garage for overflow from their flea-market purchases. Emily and Sharon often complained about the cars in the Blodgett driveway. "Why can't these people use their garage for their cars, like the other residents of the community?" Sharon asked on more than one occasion.

Maude waited patiently in the dark. Her patience soon was rewarded. The mouse had no chance. Maude carried the carcass back home. She scratched on the kitchen door. Max supported the scratching with barks. Sharon arrived to let Maude into the kitchen. Maude proudly released the dead mouse. She indicated that "The Exterminator" was on the job and that the mousetrap was superfluous.

Sharon brushed the dead mouse onto a dustpan and conveyed it to the garbage can in the garage, On her return to the kitchen she praised Maude for her diligence in protecting the family. She then made a ceremonial presentation of three "Temptations (tuna flavor)". However, Sharon left the cheese-loaded mousetrap in place.

This gave Max a wicked idea. He waited until Maude had entered the bedroom upstairs. He heard the bedroom door close, imprisoning Maude for the night. Max paused for reflection. He told himself that he really liked Maude and that he wanted her to feel good about herself. But an opportunity for creative mischief was at hand. Max could not resist.

He tapped the bar of the mousetrap. It snapped shut. Max then dislodged the small piece of cheddar with his tongue. It was a mere tidbit, but tasty nevertheless.

The next morning Emily noticed that the mousetrap had been sprung. However, there was no dead mouse present. Moreover, the bait had disappeared. "We are dealing with one clever mouse," she declared. Max turned his smile into a yawn when Maude glanced at him.

Sharon reset the trap, this time making sure that the cheddar would not be easily dislodged. That evening Maude persuaded Max to share sentry duty with her. Max was to take the first watch, pretending to be asleep on his bed in the kitchen. Maude would catch forty winks upstairs and then return to take the second watch.

Maude went into protest mode when Emily closed the bedroom door behind them. "What's wrong, Maude?" Emily asked. Maude began to dance in circles in front of the door. Emily then caught on. "Maude wants to be able to descend to the kitchen just in case 'mighty mouse' returns," she told Sharon. "Needless to say Maude has no confidence that Max would be able to catch the mouse. I'll leave the door open for her."

Maude enjoyed sleeping on the bed between Sharon and Emily. Sometimes there was no "between" available. This was not one of those times. Maude curled up on the bed and fell asleep at once. A loud "crack" from the kitchen awakened her. Maude charged downstairs, only to find the room empty except for Max. Max appeared to be asleep on his bed.

"Max, you dolt, did you not hear the mousetrap spring shut? You are supposed to be on watch, remember? The trap has been sprung, but there is no mouse. However, this time the cheese is still in the trap. I guess 'mighty mouse' didn't have enough time to eat it after springing the trap," Maude said sarcastically. She turned a steely eye on Max. "I smell a rat here, and it exudes dog-breath."

"Well, OK, but you have to admit I had you going there for a while, Maude," said Max.

"Max, do you think I would put you on sentry duty if I really believed there was a mouse to be caught?"

Freedom and its Consequences

The members of the Smith-Grabowski family were watching the televised sheepherding competition from Scotland. "It looks like this dog has a problem," Maude observed. The border collie in question and the sheep he was attempting to move appeared to be in a standoff. The collie was in a determined crouch, but there was no movement of sheep. "If I were in charge," said Max, "those sheep would be running into the pen."

"Max, you may have missed your calling," Maude said. "But how would you manage a clowder of cats?"

Max was confused. "A what?"

"A clowder," Maude replied. "It's like a herd."

Max was still confused. "What is it you heard?" he asked.

"Listen, did you ever run with a pack?" Maude asked.

"Sure," said Max.

"Well, a clowder of cats, and a herd of cows, are like a pack of dogs."

"Oh, I see," Max replied. "You are so good at explaining things."

Meanwhile, the border collie had won the battle of wills. The sheep were moving in the indicated direction. An aura of approval prevailed in the Smith-Grabowski living room. Max adopted what he took to be a "border-collie crouch". He approached Maude. "Get real," Maude said, as she prepared to leap onto a nearby chair.

"But Maude," Max objected, "To develop my herding technique I need to practice. There are no sheep around."

"You already excel at household security and homeland security. Your drug-detection skills are legendary."

"I know," Max replied, "but I envision myself as a Renaissance Dog, proficient at every undertaking of which a dog is capable. Success at sheepherding is part of this ideal."

The next morning, Emily and Sharon were enjoying coffee after breakfast. Emily called attention to the damage Max and Maude had inflicted on both sides of the kitchen door. "They scratch to go out, and they scratch to come in," she said. "I think it's time to repaint the door."

Sharon thought about that for a bit. "You know, a more permanent solution would be to install a 'pet flap' at the bottom of the door. Max and Maude then could come and go as they please. I assume that the flap would be sufficiently thick to retain reasonable insulation against the cold air in the winter."

A "pet flap" was installed later that week. Max and Maude enjoyed the new freedom it afforded. All was well until a collision took place. Maude had been outside for a period that morning. Her body told her it was time for the late-morning nap. She mounted the stone step and prepared to enter the kitchen through the flap when Max crashed through from the kitchen. Max was in high gear, in pursuit of an alien canine presence he believed to be in the backyard. In fact, the dog in question was on the sidewalk beyond the backyard. That was Max's mistake. Maude's mistake was coming in at the same time that Max was going out. Maude performed an unintended backward somersault over the step. She landed on all four paws some ten feet from the door. Maude was badly shaken, but not seriously hurt.

Maude scheduled a conference with Max to discuss how to avoid collisions in the future. "I have it," said Max, "we could adopt a rule about the use of the new pet flap. My suggestion is that the animal leaving the kitchen should have the right-of-way." Max looked pleased with himself. In his mind he had solved a knotty problem.

"That sounds good," Maude replied. "However, there is a small problem with your 'right-of-way' rule. If I am outside seeking to come in, how do I know whether you are seeking to come out at the same time?"

"You make a good point. We need a signal. I will try to remember to bark before entering or leaving the kitchen. This will alert you to wait before using the flap."

"That's very reassuring," Maude said sarcastically. "Just how good is your memory? I may not survive another collision."

"That collision was a highly improbable event," Max observed. "It is unlikely that such an event will happen again. To prevent possible collision damage in the future, I resolve to push open the flap gently upon entering or leaving. Of course, if there is some immediate threat to household security, I will have to respond quickly."

Maude ruefully concluded that an increase in freedom always comes at a price.

Maude Smith-Grabowski, Diva

Emily consulted the shopping list. One item remained, cat treats for Maude. She and Sharon headed for the pet foods section. Sharon noticed a display of catnip-flavored treats. She had read that catnip produces states of heightened awareness in 50% of adult cats. "Emily, should we see how Maude reacts to catnip?" she asked.

"OK, but you know she loves the salmon and tuna flavored treats. We should have those on hand just in case she's indifferent to catnip."

Back home, Sharon unloaded the shopping bag that contained the catnip treats. She decided to open the box to experience the catnip aroma. The treats were encased in a plastic bag. Sharon applied the kitchen scissors to the bag and noticed a slight hint of mint. "This doesn't do anything for me," she concluded.

Sharon placed the box of treats on a shelf in the cabinet above the kitchen counter. Carelessly, she left the cabinet door slightly open.

Emily suggested an afternoon nap. Sharon agreed that this was a good idea. They found Maude already asleep in the center of their bed. Sharon and Emily climbed into bed on either side of Maude. A peaceful nap was enjoyed by all.

Maude was the first to awaken. She noticed a faint, but fascinating, aroma coming from the kitchen. "This deserves investigation," she concluded. Arriving in the kitchen, she leaped onto the counter, nudged open the cabinet door, and attacked the box of catnip treats. The box fell to the counter, spilling its contents over the surface. Maude sampled one treat, then another, and then still another, ... "These are incredible," she thought.

Maude-The-Terminator morphed into Maude-The-Diva. She commanded center stage at the Metropolitan Opera. There was not an empty seat in the house. Standees occupied the spaces behind each level of seats. All eyes were on Maude.

Maude acknowledged the thunderous applause. "I will sing *Sempre libera* (forever free) from Verdi's *Tosca*, or is it Puccini's *Traviata*? No matter, it goes like this. What followed resembled the sound of nails drawn across a blackboard. Emily and Sharon quickly descended from the upstairs bedroom, hoping to intervene before Maude injured her vocal cords or the eardrums of other family members.

Emily thought to herself that the history of divas, which began with Jenny Lind, the "Swedish Nightingale," had been drawn to a close with the arrival of Maude Smith-Grabowski, the "American Blue Jay." The screeching continued. Maude seemed to be oblivious to the presence of her owners.

At this point, Max arrived home. He walked proudly into the kitchen, having received another commendation for sniffing out contraband drugs on the airport luggage carousel. Maude reacted to his arrival with enthusiasm. "Alfredo, my love. Why did I reject you? You have returned to me. Oh how I have missed you."

She returned to the aria. "*Croce e delizia*," she attempted to warble. What emerged was an ear-splitting screech.

"What is Maude doing?" Sharon asked.

Emily, a Verdi fan, explained that in this context '*croce e delizia*' means 'my love is both a cross I must bear and an ecstasy that consumes me'. "That's beautiful," Sharon replied, "but Maude has failed to express the 'agony-ecstasy' of love. What comes through are the cries of an angry blue jay."

Maude was unable to complete the aria. She descended from her catnip high very quickly. A moment later she was asleep on the kitchen floor. There were no cries of '*brava, brava*' at the end of her performance.

Emily and Sharon agreed that what remained of the catnip-laced snacks should be secured and placed in the garbage can in the garage. Maude would have to make do with salmon or tuna flavors in the future.

Max and the Bone Thief

Max consumed his breakfast Kibbles 'n Bits in record time. He moved on to his water bowl, noisily reducing the liquid level. Maude looked on impassively. She had long since given up lecturing him on proper etiquette in the consumption of food and drink.

Max left for the backyard. When he returned, Sharon applied a brush to his coat, attached his leash, and led him to her car. It was her turn to deliver Max to the local airport for drug-detection duty.

Maude decided to check the backyard for birds and chipmunks. She passed through the pet flap and was about to jump down from the back doorstep when she noticed a spray of dirt flying into the air from an area in front of the arborvitae. A large animal was hard at work digging in the Smith-Grabowski backyard. Maude turned back and reentered the kitchen. She decided to observe the evacuation project from the safety of the counter beneath the kitchen window. The animal at work in the backyard turned out to be a dog. After a while the digging ceased. The dog emerged carrying what appeared to be a bone between his teeth. "Oh, oh," said Maude to herself, "Max is not going to like this."

Max indeed was furious when he discovered the hole in the backyard. "I was saving that bone for a special occasion," he said. "Now it is gone, removed by a thief who needs to be brought to justice. What do you know about this crime, Maude?"

"Actually," Maude began, "I did happen to glance out the kitchen window while the digging was underway."

"Good work. Describe the thief," Max demanded.

"Well, you know, you've seen one dog, you've seen them all," Maude replied.

Max was annoyed. "Come on, Maude, you can do better than that. I have seen you display quite remarkable powers of observation."

"As a matter of fact, I did notice something," Maude admitted. "The culprit was blackish-brown with one white paw, the right rear I believe."

"Aha, that's Fritz," Max declared. Fritz was a member of the Polk Park Pack, the members of which acknowledged Max's alpha-status when he was in the park.

On Monday morning Max confronted Fritz in the park. They were not alone. The Polk Park Pack arrived from various locations in the park. Expectations were high. A good brawl was anticipated. The pack members were about to be disappointed.

"Oh, was that your yard?" asked Fritz. "I didn't realize."

Max was not having it. "Come on, Fritz, you haven't lost your sense of smell. My backyard is well marked. You know the bone you dug up was mine."

Fritz assumed a subservient posture. "The thing is, Max, I have these impulses from time to time. I think things are under control, but then I catch myself doing bizarre things. I don't know what came over me. I'm sorry I dug up your bone. How can I make it up to you?"

"I will expect the original bone, or a suitable replacement, by the end of the day," Max replied.

"Just place it alongside the back doorstep. Oh, and Fritz, I must compliment you on your conflict resolution skills. We dealt with this situation without violence."

The two dogs went their separate ways. Each moved away with a sense of relief.

Maude Forms a Clowder

Emily and Sharon had no plans for the holiday. Max had a suggestion. He placed himself beneath his hanging leash, and emitted a pleading whine. Emily and Sharon exchanged glances. Emily took down the leash and attached it to Max's collar. Sharon retrieved the infant carrier, placed it around her neck, gathered up Maude, and placed her inside. The Smith-Grabowski family headed for Polk Park.

Maude was content to observe activities in the park from the comfort of the infant carrier. Max immediately was joined by members of the Polk Park Pack. They set off on a circuit of the park. Near the east entrance, they observed unacceptable behavior by a male dog who was not a member of the pack. This dog had approached a four-year-old girl who was licking the ice cream in a cone she held. He barked loudly and the frightened girl dropped the cone. The dog ignored her screams and consumed the fallen ice cream.

Max was outraged. He charged the miscreant, barking loudly. The intruder locked up. He was a large dog of mixed breed. He regarded Max and assessed his chances in combat. His assessment was cut short by a further observation. The pack had followed Max and clearly shared his point of view. Terror replaced calculation. The intruder challenged the land-speed record on his departure from the park. Applause arose from park-bench occupants who had witnessed the episode.

Maude was impressed by the power of collective action. She asked herself, "why not create a similar force for good among cats?"

* * * * *

Maude arched her back to achieve her full height. She spoke to the assembled cats—Frieda, Fluffy, Ronny and Sheba. "I am pleased to open the first meeting of the Upper Millwood Benevolent Association of Cats, known informally as UMBAC," she began. "The aim of our organization is to promote, through joint action, the well-being of area cats, and consequently the general good. I propose that we adopt a mission statement. This statement lists the objectives of the organization."

"Number one: to exchange information on bird and chipmunk activity." Maude looked up from her notes. "Where is Frieda?" she asked. It turns out that Frieda was rubbing her side against the back tire of Sharon's bicycle. "Over here, Frieda," Maude commanded. The clowder was re-established.

"Number two: to share information about the presence and disposition of dogs in our area."

"Number three: to respond to . . . Where is Fluffy?" Fluffy had found a suitable urination location behind an arborvitae. Task completed, she wandered off toward home, having forgotten why she was in the Smith-Grabowski backyard. "Fluffy, get back here," Maude demanded. "As I was saying, objective number three is to respond to any complaints about mistreatment of our members."

"Number four: to organize trips to Fletcher's Fish Market to coincide with the daily discarding of fish parts. The resident bully, The Baron, is currently hobbled by leg injuries."

There were murmurs of approval from some members of the clowder. Sheba, however, was in pursuit of a butterfly in the southwest corner of the backyard. Her absence had not been noticed. Ronny expressed concern about the Fletcher's project. "I know there is strength in numbers," she said, "but The Baron is a brute and a sadist."

"Very true," Maude replied, " but remember it was my Max who disabled The Baron. With me as leader of the clowder, The Baron will not dare attack us. He knows that I can sic Max on him."

The next day, Maude led the clowder to the delivery area behind Fletcher's. The Baron hissed at them. Members of the clowder sprinted off in various directions. A disconsolate Maude returned to the Smith-Grabowski kitchen.

Maude called for an afternoon meeting of UMBAC. Only Ronny showed up, and she hurriedly left the backyard when Max crashed through the pet flap. Max had heard about the trip to Fletcher's. "Do you want me to escort you on your next visit?" he asked Maude.

"I appreciate the offer,. I really do," Maude replied, "but I realize now that a clowder is just a group of cats. There is no unity, no structure, within the group. And there clearly is no recognition of a proper exercise of leadership. As the saying goes, 'you just can't herd cats.'"

The Saga of Sid the Squirrel

Emily shared Maude's interest in birds. They both liked to have birds around in the winter. Emily watched them through binoculars. Maude stalked them in her role as escaped jungle predator.

A pole-mounted bird feeder had been delivered early in the morning. Emily placed it on a corner of the patio in the backyard, anchoring its base with two cinder blocks.

"What are you putting in the feeder?" Maude asked.

"It's Twitchell's Premium Birdsong Mixture," Emily replied.

"I didn't know that birds were cannibals," Max observed. Max received no smiles, only a stony silence.

"You know, Max, dog humor has a limited appeal," Maude said.

That afternoon, Emily looked out the kitchen window. A large squirrel was attempting to climb up the rod that supported the feeder. Sid failed on several attempts. He was persistent, however. Sid finally reached the feeder and began to remove its contents.

Emily alerted Maude to this situation. Maude passed through the pet flap. The squirrel, having consumed half the seeds in the feeder, leaped down and fled the yard.

Emily and Sharon discussed the squirrel problem over dinner. Sharon recalled that a neighbor had solved a similar problem by installing a "squirrel prevention" disk around the pole beneath the feeder. When a squirrel shimmied up the pole, he was thwarted by the disk, which prevented further ascent. Moreover, if a squirrel jumped up to land on the disk, it collapsed, causing the squirrel to fall to the ground.

The next day Emily placed a disk on the feeder pole. Sid was temporarily thwarted. Each ascent of the pole was blocked. Sid returned to the ground, apparently immersed in thought. "Aha," he said to himself. He climbed up a drainpipe to the roof of the house, scampered down to the ledge above the kitchen window, and leaped onto the feeder, grasping it in a "bear-hug." He consumed a large portion of its contents.

Maude jumped up to her kitchen observation post. She spotted Sid busily at work on the bird feeder. She quickly descended and entered the backyard through the pet flap. Sid leaped down and fled the premises. Maude was amazed that he could move so swiftly, given the weight of seeds he had consumed.

Maude spent the rest of the morning devising plans to defeat Sid. Max volunteered to provide "muscle." "There he is now," Maude announced. Max charged through the pet flap into the backyard. He announced impending mayhem with a series of barks. Sid zigged and zagged, disappearing behind the yard's single maple tree. Max came thundering around the tree. Sid was not there. Max heard sounds of claws scraping tree bark and looked up. Sid was on the first branch, looking down on Max with disdain. He knew that dogs were clumsy and that they could not climb trees.

Max retired to the kitchen. He apologized for failing to catch Sid. "Maude," he said, "some animals are climbers, and some are not. You are a cat. You can climb. I propose that I stand beneath the tree while you climb it and knock Sid to the ground. There is no other tree to which Sid can leap."

"I dunno, Max," Maude replied, "I'm out of practice at tree climbing. Sid would just move from branch to branch. I could not catch him. Even worse, he might choose not to run. What then? That is one big squirrel."

"OK, how about this?" Max began. "We attack Sid when he is most vulnerable—in mid-flight."

"I don't know how to operate a drone," Maude replied.

"No drone is needed. I just need you to warn me when Sid is about to leap toward the feeder. I will do the rest."

Maude began a watch from her kitchen window location. She was waiting for the sound of Sid's feet on the ledge above. "There he is," she said to herself.

Maude gave the order, "Now, Max!"

Max was in full barking mode even before leaving the pet flap. Sid was startled by the noise. He miscalculated his trajectory, bouncing off the feeder to the ground.

Max had Sid's tail before Sid could escape. Max performed his best discus-throwing imitation. He swung Sid around in a counter-clockwise loop, gaining momentum during the circuit. Max proceeded into a second revolution, releasing Sid's tail at the halfway point.

Sid landed halfway up one of the arborvitae at the edge of the backyard. Max waited at the base of the tree for a while, growling softly. There was no motion from the branches above. Max soon grew tired of this waiting game. He lifted his right rear leg and left a message on the trunk of the tree for any incautious intruding squirrels. Back inside, Max added "squirrel removal expertise" to his resume.

Sid and his confederates bypassed the Smith-Grabowski residence for the remainder of the winter. Songbirds returned to the feeder, providing Emily with entries for her notebook and Maude with visions of pursuit and capture. Fortunately for the birds, Maude's success rate at converting visions into actual captures remained at zero.

A-Tenting We Will Go

The Smith-Grabowski family drove to the nearby state park They took possession of an isolated tent site. Maude was the last to emerge from the tent in the morning. She had not slept well. Emily was cooking sausages over a charcoal fire. Max was by her side, drooling copiously. Sharon was grating cheese into a bowl of well-whisked eggs.

Max downed his portion of the sausages in two gulps. Maude began yet another lecture on the proper consumption and enjoyment of food, but then said "Oh, forget it, Max. Dogs will be dogs."

Breakfast concluded, Sharon proposed a walk into the surrounding woods. Everyone was on board, if 'on board' includes being placed in Emily's infant carrier. Maude found that she could catnap even though Emily was in motion.

After ten minutes the group came upon a small lake. Sharon threw a large stick into the lake for Max to fetch. Max jumped in, anxious to show off his retrieving skills. Moments later he dropped the stick in front of Sharon, pausing to shake the water from his coat. Sharon did not retreat in time. Max barked to indicate he was ready for the next toss. "No more, Max," Sharon said. "I need to dry off."

Emily proposed that they continue the hike. Sharon volunteered to lead. The Smith-Grabowski family turned away from the lake and re-entered the woods. A half hour later the group stopped at a large flat rock. "I think it's time to go back," Emily suggested. There was general agreement to do so.

Sharon turned them around and attempted to retrace their steps. After ten minutes, Emily complained that nothing looked familiar. "I think we're lost," she said.

"You may be right," Sharon conceded. "I wish I had paid more attention to landmarks on our path away from the campsite."

Max overheard this conversation. He had been enjoying the hike, not realizing that Sharon was trying to return to the campsite. "Is there a problem?" he asked.

Emily seemed to be about to cry. "We are lost in the woods," she moaned.

Max sought to reassure her. He was confident that he could use his superior tracking skills to retrace the path back to the tent. "Don't be upset, Emily, I will use my superior tracking skills to retrace our path back to the tent," Max said confidently.

Max assumed command by trotting at the front of the group. There were so many scents to follow—mosquito repellent, deodorant, deer droppings (a misstep by Emily). Fortunately, these scents were grouped together. The retracing process was easy.

Max was in the lead as the family approached the campsite. An animal blocked the way. It resembled an overgrown black squirrel with a white stripe on its back. Max invited the animal to vacate the path. The animal failed to move. Either it did not understand dog language or it refused to be bullied.

Max was outraged at this disobedience. He charged the animal, barking furiously. The animal calmly turned its back and released a spray that temporarily blinded Max. Max retreated back to Sharon and Emily. He was keenly aware that his coat now emitted a repulsive odor.

"Max, you fool," Maude admonished, "you never challenge a skunk. They have these 'skunk glands' that they use to squirt nasty fluid on you." Max complained that this advice would have been more useful before the encounter with the skunk.

"What are we going to do?" Emily asked. "There is no way to give Max a bath here."

"True enough," Sharon replied, "but remember how much Max enjoyed retrieving sticks from the lake earlier. The lake is only ten minutes away, and there is shampoo in the car."

Emily was in agreement. "Good plan.".

The family set forth again along the path to the lake. Max was encouraged to lead at a point twenty yards in advance. When the lake came into view, Max began to jump up and down. It was strange. He hated baths. "Getting wet just for the sake of it is stupid," he thought.

"But getting wet in the course of a game of fetch is a different matter. It allows me to exhibit my swimming and retrieving skills."

Emily tossed a stick into the lake. Max jumped in after it, paddling furiously. He brought the stick back, not to Emily, but to Sharon. Max knew that Sharon was the more athletic of the two. She would throw the stick much further. Max enjoyed a challenge.

He did not enjoy what happened next. Emily grabbed him from behind and doused him with shampoo. "This is not part of the game," he protested. However, when Sharon let fly a mighty toss into the lake, Max went after it. The toss, capture, and retrieve sequence was repeated several times. Max was panting heavily when Sharon announced that the game was over and that Max was the undisputed champion of stick retrieval. Max responded by shaking himself vigorously. "If I have to get wet, everyone gets wet," he said to himself. The Smith-Grabowski family then returned to their campsite.

Despite the shampoo-and-water treatment, Max still smelled strongly of skunk. Sharon consulted Emily. "Is this the end of our camping trip?" she asked. "I don't think we could bear sharing a tent with Max in his present condition."

"Another night camping is out of the question," Emily replied. "Let's pack up and return home. We can quarantine Max in the basement while we seek further anti-skunk-odor treatments."

"There is a karmic unbalance in my universe, Maude," Max said ruefully. "Somewhere out there is a skunk who needs to be punished. I heard Sharon say that skunks hate strong odors. Imagine that. Odors other than their own, I take it. What I need is a bottle of garlic juice and a water pistol."

"But how will you identify the skunk who sprayed you?" Maude said. "He or she was a completely undistinguished member of the species."

"That is a problem," Max agreed. "For karmic balance I might need to spray a dozen or so skunks."

"You have a weird sense of karmic balance," Maude said. "Fortunately this discussion is academic. There is no way you could discharge a water pistol with your paws."

Max Loves Patty

"The Giants are playing Dallas on Monday Night Football. I will be in the den," Clarence (Chip) Harwood announced.

"Football, ugh. That's all you ever watch," his wife Bertha replied.

"Well, if the Giants-Cowboys game doesn't interest you, you have a widescreen TV in your bedroom," was the unsympathetic rejoinder.

Bertha had been Chip's nurse at Millwood Hospital during his convalescence from heart surgery. Chip persuaded her to come home with him as a highly-paid nurse-companion. One month later, Bertha suggested that to "save appearances" she should become "Mrs. Harwood." Chip had no objection, provided she sign a very restrictive pre-nuptial agreement. The agreement required Bertha's continuing presence *chez* Harwood as a condition of inheritance.

Bertha was becoming itchy. She needed to get away from confinement in the Harwood Mansion. At breakfast she listened dutifully to Chip's replay of the Giants' victory. She then floated the idea of a vacation in a warmer clime. Bertha suggested Cancun, the Bahamas, and even Florida as desirable locations for sun and fun.

Chip wasn't interested. He had everything he needed here in Millwood. "I'm sorry, Bertie," he said. "I need to regain my strength. I have not recovered the stamina I had before the operation. I still require a walker to get around." What Chip was thinking was that the playoffs began next week. Who knew if these games were televised in Cancun or the Bahamas. And even if they were televised down there, who wanted to watch the games on a hotel room TV screen?

The next day, Bertha placed a call to her sister Ann in Atlanta. "Ann," she pleaded, " I gotta get outta here." Could you call and leave a message saying that you had a high-ankle sprain and need me to come down to help out for a few days." Ann did as requested. Bertha was on a plane to Atlanta later in the day.

Chip was indifferent to her departure. The following day was sunny, a pleasant change after three days of rain. He decided to walk out to the sidewalk and back. A flight of geese made a noisy intrusion in the sky above. Chip looked up, marveling at the nearly perfect "V" that was formed.

This was a mistake. He rolled the left wheel of the walker off the macadam onto the rain-soaked adjoining grass. The walker, and Chip with it, tumbled over. Chip felt a sharp pain in his left ankle, which had followed the left wheel off the driveway. He lay on his side moaning as Max came along on the sidewalk.

Max had been at the park with Sharon. Sharon had entered into a deep discussion with a coworker. Max was anxious to leave. Sharon, noting this, told him to return home by himself. She would meet him there later.

Max trotted off, deciding to follow an interesting aroma that led past the Harwood Mansion. It took him a bit out of the way, but he thought it might lead to a new adventure. It certainly did. He heard the moans coming from the Harwood driveway. Max ran to the fallen Chip, barking softly to let him know that he was on the scene and that everything would be OK.

Max gave Chip's hand a reassuring lick and ran rapidly to the front door of the mansion. He barked loudly while running in a small circle. There was no response from within. Housekeeper Jennifer was not due to report until noon.

Perhaps there are people on the sidewalk, Max thought. He ran quickly to that location. There was no one in sight. There were cars passing, however. Max went into his barking-while-turning-in-a-circle routine. A passing patrol car pulled over. Max encouraged the female officer who emerged from the passenger-side door to follow him. Upon spotting Chip, Officer Brandon called for an ambulance. Chip asked her to make a note of the name and address on Max's dog tag.

Chip returned home the next day in an ankle boot and a wheelchair. He called the Smith-Grabowski residence. "Ms. Smith," he began, " your dog Max saw to it that I received needed care after I fell in my driveway. I very much would like to thank him. Could you bring him over this morning? I have a treat for him." Emily thanked Chip for informing her of Max's latest act of heroism. She agreed to drop off Max at 11 o'clock, promising to return at 12.

"Max, my great friend, it's good to see you," Chip said. "Sit down, I have a treat for you." Max obediently sat down in front of Chip's wheelchair. He extended his right paw as well. Chip could not reach it. Max issued a soft bark, indicating that he knew how to fix this. He moved to the side of the chair, sat down, and again extended his paw. "What an intelligent dog," Chip said as he shook Max's paw. Max smiled modestly.

Jennifer arrived with a jar and some crackers. Chip opened the jar. "Oh, this is heaven," Max thought, as the aroma from the open jar reached him. Chip spread pâté on a cracker and extended it to Max.

Max recalled numerous lectures from Maude about savoring food. He gently closed his teeth on the cracker and allowed it to remain in his mouth all of two seconds before swallowing. His stomach sent messages of "bravo" to his brain. He was in love with this man Chip. "How can I express this love?" he wondered. "What would Maude do? Ah, I have it," he concluded. Max produced his best imitation of Maude purring. It was a low growl. Nevertheless, Chip caught the appreciation it expressed. He prepared another cracker-with-pâté.

After returning home, Max related to Maude that "Chip gave me the most delicious snack. It has a silky texture ideal for spreading on crackers. He referred to it as 'patty da frog grass', or something like that. What do you know about this delicacy?"

"Nothing, I'm afraid, but I'll ask my friend Helene. She is French. She will know all about this 'patty da frog grass'".

Maude reported back later in the day. "According to Helene," Maude related, "'pâté de foie gras' is goose liver pâté. Apparently French farmers force-feed geese to enlarge their livers. They then kill the geese and market their livers. Animal rights activists have protested this practice, but the French argue that the geese are quite content with this arrangement."

"Pâté de foie gras," Max repeated. "If there were gods, this is what they would eat."

On the way back from the park later that week, Max tugged on his leash in the direction of the Harwood Mansion. "OK, Max, we can return home that way," said Emily.

Max hoped that his great friend Chip would be outside. Indeed he was, moving slowly behind his walker toward the sidewalk. He was accompanied by his wife Bertha, who had returned from a visit with her sister in Atlanta. Bertha had found that life with sister was even more suffocating than life with Chip. At Harwood Mansion she had space to herself and a housekeeper to supervise. Moreover, she now had a cocker spaniel named Rusty. Rusty currently was straining on his leash as he directed a volley of irritating barks at Max.

Chip recognized Max. He welcomed him warmly, calling upon Rusty to "shut the hell up." Max responded to the annoying spaniel with "barks of eternal friendship." Rusty ignored this, continuing to yap away.

Max did not wish to cause trouble for his friend Chip. This spaniel was insufferable, but it now was his turf. Max recognized the canine imperative, "respect the home territory of other dogs." He turned away, moving back to the sidewalk.

Back home, Emily praised Max. "You were the bigger dog, Max. You could have dismembered that yappy spaniel, but instead you honored your friendship with Mr. Harwood." Max accepted the compliment with a grateful smile.

Max observed that Emily was beginning to prepare lunch. Lunch was a tradition among human beings. Max found this unfair to dogs. He was fed just twice a day. Why was there no lunchtime for dogs? Perhaps Emily would deliver a small snack, at least.

Did Emily read his mind? She announced that she had a special treat for him. "Could it be?" Max wondered. Indeed it could. Emily had purchased a jar of pâté de foie gras. Max felt his love for Emily grow to new heights.

He completely forgot Maude's instructions on dining etiquette as he downed the cracker-with-pâté in record time.

Trouble at Polk Park

"Have you lost your nose, Max? This is the third session in a row with no drugs discovered on the airport luggage carousel." Max was uncertain whether Officer Heinz was teasing. He growled softly. "Or perhaps the bad guys have learned about your incredible detection skills and have chosen other ways to transport their drugs." Max barked to indicate agreement. "That is the only reasonable conclusion," he said to himself. Heinz stopped the car in front of the Smith-Grabowski residence. He gave Max a dog biscuit and told him he looked forward to working with him again next weekend.

Maude met Max as he came through the pet flap. "Good, you're home," she said.

"Did you miss me, Maude?" Max asked.

"Don't be naive," was the rejoinder. "There was an intruder in the backyard while you were at work. Much barking. I was afraid he would come through the flap into the kitchen. I chose to retreat to the upstairs bedroom. When I looked out the window, the dog had left."

"It's all right, I will investigate," Max said as he left for the backyard. He returned shortly thereafter. "It was Prince," he reported. "He left me a message to contact him. I will head over to his house to see if he is outside."

Max found Prince on a chain linked to a stake in his backyard. He looked awful. "Prince, old buddy, what happened?" Max asked.

"Max, there has been a revolution at the park. A large mutt named Samson has taken over leadership of the Polk Park Pack. He and his followers have been intimidating parkgoers and terrorizing their children. Samson is one mean mutt."

"Members of the pack respected your leadership," Prince said. "I was honored to deputize for you in your absence. I thought that they would support me against this intruder. But they left me to face him alone. I tried to stop him, but he was too big and strong. He is now in control of the park and I am confined to my home until my bite wounds heal."

The next day Max confronted Samson in the park. He informed Samson that he, Max, was leader of the Polk Park Pack, and that Prince was acting alpha-dog in his absence."

"Yeah," said Samson. "That was yesterday. Today I am in charge. If you don't like it, we can fight for alpha-status right now."

"I don't think that's a good idea," Max said. "Do you see that woman on the bench behind us?"

"Yeah, so what?" Samson replied.

"She has come to the park from target practice," Max stated. "She bought a gun yesterday and she loves using it. It's in her bag now. If we fight, she will take it out and shoot you. I don't like you, but I don't want to be responsible for your death."

Samson initially was skeptical. But then he noticed a steely glare in her eyes as Sharon looked at him. While Samson hesitated, Max proposed an alternative. "Let's have a competition to decide who is top dog. The top dog should be the strongest, fastest and best jumper. Don't you agree?"

"Yeah, that sounds right," Samson replied.

"Good," Max said. "I propose three contests. The first dog to win two of these contests becomes alpha-dog in the park. The first contest is a race around the park. The second is a jump over a park bench. And the third contest is a tug-of-war with you and me grasping the opposite ends of a knotted rope."

"You might as well concede now. There is no way you could beat me at any of these contests," Samson boasted.

"OK, let's get started," said Max. "The race will be one lap around the park, passing on the outside of the three benches at its corners."

Max surveyed the course. He noted that there were wet leaves under the third bench. "Now if these leaves extend behind the bench," he thought, "I may win this race."

Max was fast. Samson appeared to be faster. Samson was first to round both the first bench and the second bench. Max swung wide at the second bench. It appeared to Samson that Max was trying to pass him on the outside. "That won't work," Samson said to himself. "I'll stay on the inside rounding the third bench. He will have too far to go to pass me."

Samson didn't notice the leaves behind the third bench until it was too late. He tried to turn left around the bench but instead skidded on the leaves into the fence beyond. Max, having circled wide around the bench, coasted to victory.

"This is absurd," said Samson. "Everyone saw that I am faster than you. If it had not been for those leaves, I would have been an easy winner."

"Sorry, Samson," Max replied, "The winner of a race is the first to cross the finish line. That was me."

Samson glowered at Max. "There's no way you can beat me at jumping or feats of strength. Let's get on with it," he growled.

Max gestured toward a park bench. Its back was about three feet high. "Samson, the object is to get over the back of the bench to the ground behind it. It doesn't matter if you touch the bench on the way over. What counts is getting over the bench. Since you lost the first contest, you get to go first."

Samson took a long run toward the bench. He soared into the air. Alas, he began to soar too soon. When he reached the top of the bench he already was descending. Both front paws struck the top of the bench. He fell back, striking the seat of the bench before bouncing to the ground. "Oh, you were so close," Max sympathized. "Are you all right?"

Samson was far from all right. "I'm in pain. My ribs are sore, and I cannot put any pressure on my front paws," he complained. "But I can't wait to see what happens on your jump."

"Watch this," said Max confidently. He walked up to the bench and jumped easily onto its seat. He then placed his front paws on its back and propelled himself onto the ground behind. "That's two wins for me," Max announced, "It is all well and good to be fast and strong, Samson, but it's brains that count in the last analysis. I am the alpha-dog at Polk Park."

Samson had nothing to say.

The dogs assembled to watch the contest had little hope that the tyrant would be defeated. They were elated when Max emerged the victor. The pack members pledged their allegiance to the restored Max - Prince dynasty.

At the Beach

Max preceded Emily and Sharon into the two-room cabin set upon a sand dune overlooking the ocean. The women began to unpack. Max was excited. "I do enjoy going to new places and finding new things to do," he announced to Maude.

"I respect your enthusiasm," Maude replied, "but I would prefer to remain at home. I know where everything is there, including various hiding places to avoid unpleasant guests. Why go elsewhere?"

"Maude, you are a wet blanket," Max said. He then noted a smoky marijuana odor. It was coming from a wastebasket in the bathroom. Max placed his nose over the rim of the basket and barked loudly. Emily came to investigate. She found the remains of a reefer stuck to some chewing gum at the bottom of the basket. She praised Max on its detection, as she relocated it in a garbage can outside.

Ten minutes later, Sharon and Emily, sporting colorful bikinis, headed across the sand to the edge of the ocean. Max leaped happily alongside. He enjoyed the warmth and resilience of the sand. Maude elected to watch their activities from the front window of the cabin.

"Ooh, this is different," Max noted. "The water has a salty taste, quite unlike lake water. This is great." He joined Sharon as she waded out into the surf. The water seemed to be resisting him. "It's a good thing I am a strong swimmer," he thought.

Suddenly he was not thinking at all. What he took to be a ripple in the ocean beyond developed into a sizeable wave. It slammed into Max as it unfurled toward the beach. For an instant he was submerged beneath the wave. Its impact spun him around. He allowed himself to be carried toward the beach by the wave. "Oh, this is fun," he declared. There was an apparently endless succession of waves in the ocean. Max discovered that by paddling outward from the shore he then could ride an incoming wave. He loved the feeling of weightlessness as he was carried along by a wave.

Back in the cabin, he tried to interest Maude in sharing this experience. "I prefer to watch the action from the security of the cabin," she said. "I have no interest in getting my fur wet. Moreover, the sand is too hot. I have sensitive paws."

The next morning, there was a knock on the cabin door. Betty Strong, from the cabin next door, was in tears. Lizzie, her Siamese, had pushed open the screen door and disappeared. The night had been warm and the Strongs had left the cabin door open without latching the screen door. Betty asked Emily and Sharon to be on the lookout for Lizzie.

Sharon asked if Betty had brought a toy or bed that Lizzie used. "Why, we always bring her bed on trips," Betty said.

Max moved to Sharon's side and looked up expectantly. "Max here is a drug-detecting professional," Sharon said. "He might be able to locate Lizzie if he is exposed to her scent. "

"I am most grateful," said Betty, smiling at Max. "Let me bring over Lizzie's bed. Perhaps Max will be able to discover where she has gone."

Max realized that a game of "tracking the cat" was afoot. He committed the cat-bed scent to memory and emerged from the cabin. Max moved along the beach from east to west and back again. There was no match for the cat-bed scent. "Maude hates the sandy beach," he recalled. "Perhaps Lizzie decided to move away from the sand."

Max headed inland. There were several more-substantial houses on higher ground. Each of these houses rested on stilts, for protection from storm surges. "Aha," said Max, as he encountered the cat-bed scent. He discovered Lizzie. She was asleep underneath one of the elevated houses. There was a dead mouse nearby.

Max elected not to bark to announce his discovery. He feared Lizzie would be frightened by the sounds of a strange dog. Instead he returned to Sharon and Betty, nudged Sharon's leg and turned back toward the house that sheltered Lizzie.

Lizzie looked out from under the house as they approached. She recognized Betty at once. Lizzie picked up the recently terminated mouse. She proudly deposited the carcass at Betty's feet. Betty gathered Lizzie into her arms, enveloping her in a fierce hug. She heaped praise on Max, locating him in the pantheon of super-heroes.

That evening there was a knock on the cabin door. Max prepared to respond, despite being very tired from an afternoon of wave-riding. But then he recognized a favorite aroma—pepperoni pizza. He remained on guard, but raised no objection to the appearance of a stranger holding a pizza box. "Courtesy of your neighbors, the Strongs," the stranger said. Max was granted three slices as a reward for winning the "tracking the cat" game.

A Visit from Rose Grabowski

Sharon was about to pour herself a glass of wine when the front doorbell rang. "Who could that be at 5 o'clock in the afternoon?" she wondered. Then it came to her. "Aha, of course," she said. She prepared a polite but dismissive response to the ubiquitous white-shirted men who would ask, "Have you heard the good news?" Sharon peeked out the viewing eyepiece in the front door. If only it had been two men in white shirts.

It was her mother.

"Mother, how great to see you," Sharon exclaimed. Rose reported that she had accompanied Frank to a convention of Rotarians in Ferndale, just 50 miles away. "I was so bored," she complained. "There were no organized activities for spouses. So I said to myself, 'Why not drive over to see my baby?'"

Max, who had just entered the kitchen *via* the pet flap, heard Rose's voice. He executed a 180-degree turn. Max suddenly had remembered an urgent need to relocate the bone he had buried last week.

"You must be tired from the drive, Mother. Come join me in the kitchen. I'll make you one of your favorite vodka martinis."

Rose was halfway through her drink when Emily arrived. After exchanging pleasantries with Rose, Emily excused herself "to get into something more comfortable".

Emily was in panic mode. If Rose came upstairs she would discover the Sharon-Emily sleeping arrangement. Emily quickly relocated hand cream, a water glass, and her pajamas to the guest bedroom. Fortunately, her clothes already were stored in the guest bedroom. She and Sharon had accumulated too much clothing to be stored in just one bedroom. Emily exchanged her business suit and blouse for slacks and a sweater. She left the business outfit displayed conspicuously over an armchair. Emily then rejoined Sharon and Rose in the kitchen. She offered to take over dinner preparation so Sharon could visit with her mother in the living room.

Maude sensed the tension that Rose had created. She heard Emily ask Sharon "Is she planning to stay overnight?"

"God, I hope not," Sharon replied. Maude strolled into the living room, issued a greeting to Rose, and leaped onto the sofa beside her. Rose paid no attention. Maude advanced to Rose's lap, emitting an anticipatory purr. Rose shoved her away. Maude persisted, rubbing her back against Rose's thigh. Rose found it difficult to present a coherent lecture on the topic of matrimony. "Can't you do something about the cat?" she pleaded.

Sharon removed Maude to the kitchen. Maude picked up her cloth mouse and returned to the living room. She dropped the mouse on Rose's shoes, looking up for praise. "She really likes you, Mom," Sharon said. "I've never seen her do that for anyone else."

"I don't care," Rose replied, "it's very annoying."

Maude was carried out to the kitchen once again. "Max," she pleaded, "see what you can do to hasten her departure." Max was unsure how to accomplish this. He began with a persistent offering of his right paw. There was no response from Rose. Rose had switched the conversation to Sharon's romantic life. Sharon made vague references to several prospects in her office.

Emily announced that dinner was ready. Rose was seated first. Maude approached at once, rubbing her side against Rose's left leg. Max placed his jaw on Rose's right thigh, drooling freely. Rose again demanded that the animals be banished. "It is amazing how Max and Maude have taken to you," Sharon said, "they really are glad to see you."

Over coffee, Rose weighed her options. The first was a short drive back to the convention. There she would get to hear Frank's summary of the day's meetings. The second was a night spent repelling the advances of these obnoxious animals. Max helped her make the right choice. He visited his water bowl and then slobbered over her shoes.

Max and Maude accompanied Rose to the front door, as if unwilling to let her leave. Maude emitted a plaintive cry. Max produced a whine that could pass for a sob. Rose embraced Sharon, said goodbye to Emily, and removed her leg from Max's grasp. She reached her car with a sense of relief.

The remaining family members regrouped in the kitchen. Sharon said that she never had been so proud of Max and Maude. She reached for the salmon-flavored treats and the pâté de foie gras.

A No-Drug Zone

Max arrived at Polk Park for a 3:30 romp with his pack. Greetings were exchanged. Max led the pack on a circuit of the park. At the southeast corner, a short, bald man claimed the bench located there. Doug "Digger" Dimwell removed the running shoes from around his neck. He placed them next to the gym bag on the bench.

Students at the nearby high school had been dismissed for the day. Some took a path through the park on their way home. A group of three left the path to converse with Digger. Digger unzipped his gym bag as the students surrounded him. An exchange of some sort then took place. The students returned to the path with a spring to their steps.

Max had observed this from afar. Upon approaching Digger's corner he caught the aroma of a substance he was trained to detect. It appeared to emanate from Digger's gym bag. Max was unsure about what to do. Officer Oliver was not beside him, ready to confiscate the drugs.

Two male students left the path and headed toward Digger. Max noticed this. He had an idea. "Prince, Ralph, Andy, Spot, Zeno, let's form a barrier around that bench. If anyone approaches Digger, we will bark and growl at them." This tactic proved effective. Students passing through the park wanted no part of the Polk Park Pack.

Digger was not pleased. These mutts were affecting business. Sensing that Max was their leader, he aimed a kick at him. Max ducked, swiveled his head around, and clamped down on Digger's ankle. He was careful not to break the skin. Max issued a warning growl as he released the ankle. Digger decided to leave the park. Max and the pack followed him to the park exit.

Max said goodbye to his mates. He headed home, proud of the accomplishments of the day.

The next day was a work day. Officer Oliver picked up Max at 9 o'clock. Prince was in charge at the park. That afternoon Digger returned to his bench. He was doing a modest amount of business, despite the fact that the high school was closed for the weekend. Prince noticed this. He alerted the other pack members. Prince proposed that they surround Digger, just as they had done the previous day.

As the pack approached, Digger removed a large object from his bag. It was a toy water cannon, loaded with a quart of ammonia solution. The pack took up positions around the bench. Digger yelled to get the dogs to turn toward him. He then discharged the water cannon. Prince and the others turned away, howling. They rubbed their eyes with their paws. This did not help. The ammonia produced pain that subsided only after the shedding of copious tears. The pack disbanded. There were no further interruptions of Digger's drug business.

Prince, half-blinded by the ammonia spray, retreated to Max's house. He lay down on the grass in front of the back door, whimpering softly.

Max was surprised to see him. "What's wrong, Prince?" he asked. Prince recounted the spraying incident at the park. He complained about a stinging sensation in his eyes. "Perhaps a water bath would help," Max thought. He brought Prince inside. Max bypassed his water bowl as too shallow. "I've got it,", he said. Max nudged open the door of the downstairs bathroom.

"Really, do you think that will help?" Prince asked.

"Yes, go ahead," Max replied, "pretend you are bobbing for apples."

"Oh, that is better, " Prince said, shaking his head vigorously to remove excess water.

Emily was not pleased when she slipped, and almost fell, in the bathroom later. She assumed that Max was the culprit. Max received a lecture about restricting himself to the "special water" provided in his water bowl. She pointed out that this water bowl was full at present, hence there had been no need to go elsewhere. Max could not explain the injury to Prince and his attempt to provide relief. He adopted a contrite posture.

Sunday also was a work day for Max. Officer Oliver was in charge of returning Max to the Smith-Grabowski house. The trip took them along a road adjacent to Polk Park. As they approached the park, Max commenced his "drugs present" barks. "Are you sure, Max?" Oliver asked, as he slowed the car. Max produced more barks at even higher volume. "All right," Oliver said. He stopped the car and opened its back door. Before he could attach a leash, Max was in full flight across the park toward Digger.

Digger recognized him. He had invested in a can of pepper spray for such emergencies. He reached into his bag for it. But then he saw a man in uniform trying to catch up with Max. A pepper spray release now seemed to be counter-productive. He grabbed his bag, turned, and sought to flee the park.

He was no match for Max. Max caught his left leg between his jaws and held on. Digger landed face down on the park turf. "Well, well," said Oliver, as he placed handcuffs on Digger, "possession with intent to distribute, and within a half mile of a school as well."

On Monday, Prince and the others asked Max about the absence of Digger from the park. Max smiled and said, "I took care of him. Nobody sprays members of my pack." Prince, Ralph, Andy, Spot and Zeno expressed their gratitude to be members of a pack that had such a courageous and effective leader.

Steve, the Real Estate Developer

Emily maneuvered her Subaru into the garage. She had not noticed the black Civic parked in front of the house. Inside, Emily exchanged greetings with Max and Maude. The front doorbell rang. Max barked to announce that inappropriate behavior would not be tolerated. Emily saw that it was her brother Steve at the door. Emily embraced Steve. Max awarded him two tail-wag thumps.

"Steve, how have you been?" Emily asked.

"I'm better now," he replied, "actually, I am off the stuff. I have found an alcohol-free beer that I like, and I bring a bottle of unsweetened cranberry juice to parties where cocktails are served. I don't miss the old days of alcoholic incoherence at all."

"That's great, Steve. Can you stay for dinner? I have a pot roast ready to put into the oven. There will be plenty of food. We can catch up with what you have been doing since we last saw you."

"I would like that, if Sharon won't mind. Actually, I was hoping you would let me crash here for a few days. My former apartment is scheduled for conversion into a condo, and the owner is repainting the place. I have to be out by the end of the month."

Sharon then entered the kitchen from the garage. Spotting Steve, she greeted him warmly. "Steve, I hope you are here for a visit," she said.

"That's very kind of you," Steve replied. "I am a bit at loose ends at present. " Emily conferred with Sharon. They agreed that Steve could occupy the guest room while he searched for a suitable replacement apartment.

Maude had been observing Steve as he sought permission to relocate to the Smith-Grabowski residence. She noted that, as he spoke, Steve shifted his weight from one foot to the other. Moreover, he directed his gaze to a point between Emily and Sharon, rather than at first one and then the other. "Aha," Maude whispered to Max, "these body movements are indicators of unease. I suspect that Steve is not telling the truth about a condo conversion."

Sharon confirmed Maude's analysis the next morning. There was no apartment-to-condominium conversion application on file for Steve's building.

"OK, Steve, what is really going on?" Emily asked. "Are you in some kind of trouble?"

"Actually, I'm trying to get away from Jennifer. She didn't react well to our recent breakup. She has been phoning at all hours and trailing me when I go out. I just need to avoid her for a while."

Maude was not having it. "Notice his eye movements and the way he folds and unfolds his hands while he talks," she said. "He is making up this 'Jennifer is a stalker' story."

"I dunno, Maude," Max replied, "Steve seems to be sincere. I think it is believable that Jennifer is pursuing him. Some human females are very possessive. Upon rejection, they become vindictive. I don't see what his eyes and hands have to do with it."

Once again, Maude was correct. That afternoon, while Emily and Sharon were at work, a man arrived at the Smith-Grabowski house. He appeared to be angry. Steve left to join him in his car. There was much shouting and hand waving. Steve returned after ten minutes. The angry stranger drove away.

That evening Steve volunteered to get food from a Thai restaurant in town. There was a phone call for him while he was out. The caller left a message. Sharon was to tell Steve that "the partnership has been dissolved and that Joe wants his money back." Sharon waited until after dinner to give Steve the message.

"What's going on, Steve?" Emily demanded.

"I got involved in a business deal that went sour," Steve replied. "I was looking for a source of income to support me while I'm working on my novel. Driving past the vacant lot along the river on the way into town, it struck me that this would be an ideal spot for a parking lot. It's only a five-minute walk to the three office buildings on Water Street. And the present owner is anxious to sell."

"Since I currently am low on cash, I decided I needed a business partner to help with start-up expenses. Joe Lathrop, an exdrinking buddy from the floor below, agreed to a 50-50 partnership. He provided the money for the Spivak Construction Company's site plan for the lot. Now he wants his money back."

"Why did Joe change his mind?" Emily asked. "Did Spivak conclude that the property is unsuitable for a parking lot?"

"No," Steve replied, "there was a different problem. There's a 19th century abandoned grist mill on the property. The Spivak plan was to raze it. It turns out, however, that the city fathers have applied for federal landmark status for the mill. If the mill is awarded this status, there is no question of a parking lot there."

This was Steve's third story to account for his presence in the Smith-Grabowski household. Maude observed that his body language and gestures remained suspect. The parking-lot story was more elaborate than the first two stories. However, it was obvious to Maude that Steve was lying. She informed Max. Max was not convinced. But then Max did not score high on Maude's perceptiveness index. "Max," Maude said, " we need to alert Emily and Sharon. Support me on this."

Maude commenced to bounce around, pretending to be gagging on a hairball. She alternated between coughs and screams. Sharon became alarmed. She picked up Maude and carried her into the kitchen. Maude then made a miraculous recovery. "I get it, Maude," Sharon said. "Well done. I agree with you. Steve can't be trusted to tell the truth." Sharon assured Maude that she understood her performance, and that she shared her point of view on Steve.

The next day Sharon cornered William ("Will") Williams, a partner in her investments firm and a member of City Council. "Will," she asked, "I understand that an application has been made to have Potter's Mill declared a national landmark. Has there been a reply?"

"What?" Will replied, "landmark status! That crumbling pile of limestone dates from 1915. It's an eyesore. Moreover, it's an accident hazard. At our last meeting we passed a condemnation resolution. It should be gone later in the week."

Sharon didn't tell Emily about the meeting. "I should save this information for an appropriate moment," she said to herself. Emily and I are driving into town and I say "I guess the city fathers decided to load Potter's Mill onto a flatbed and transfer it to a museum."

Meanwhile, Steve had cashed a check from Emily and was on route to the west coast. He was open to the new experiences that would inform his Great American Novel.

Maude Meets Her Prince

Max had left for drug-detection duty. Emily and Sharon were on a shopping trip. Maude was home alone with Prince. Prince was a house guest while his owners spent a week in Puerto Rico.

Maude had no problem with Prince. They both liked Max. And, after all, cats and dogs have different interests. Maude decided to spend some time outside. She exited the kitchen through the pet flap. Prince watched her depart. "This is strange," he thought, "when I want to go out, I bark until a person opens the door. I know how to leave around an open door, but not through a door. That is not right."

Maude returned to the kitchen. "Prince," she said, "there is an unauthorized dog in our yard. Max is not here. It's up to you to make this intruder disappear." Prince sat motionless. His head was down. He was either embarrassed or seeking spiritual guidance. "C'mon Prince," Maude urged, "surely you are not afraid of that flap."

"It's not natural," Prince replied, "you do not go through doors."

"Here, let me show you," Maude said. She left and quickly reentered. There still was no response from Prince. "OK, Prince," Maude said in desperation, "watch me. I am going to back into the flap. See how it opens when I push backward on it. If I can open it, surely you can. Your butt is much larger than mine. Give it a try."

Instead, Prince curled up in his bed next to Max's bed in the kitchen. "Discretion is the better part of valor," he thought, as he closed his eyes.

Maude went back outside. There no longer was an alien canine presence. She crawled to her favorite observation post behind the coiled garden hose. From this location, she could watch the activity at the bird feeder. Occasionally a bird would jump down from the feeder to peck at seeds that had been dislodged from the feeder. That is when Maude would spring forth from her hiding place. The birds invariably became airborne before Maude could reach them.

Maude was not discouraged by continuing failure. Her hunting heritage required persistence. "It's not whether you win or lose," she thought, "but how you play the game."

Prince couldn't sleep. There was a most interesting aroma coming from the corner of the kitchen counter. This was where Maude's feeding station was located. Could it be that she had not finished her breakfast? Prince uncoiled from his bed. He decided to investigate. It was true. There was food in Maude's dish. "I wonder how it tastes?" Prince asked himself. He used his paw to pull the dish toward the counter edge. He then sampled the cat food. "It is delicious," he concluded. "I should finish it so that Maude does not get a lecture about cleaning her plate."

Maude was not pleased to find her dish empty. "What am I supposed to do if I get peckish this afternoon?" she asked Prince.

"Peckish?" Prince queried.

"Hungry, you Nobel Laureate," Maude responded.

"I appreciate the compliment," Prince said. "We Labradors are a noble breed. But why would you be eating in mid-afternoon? Everyone knows that there is just breakfast and dinner."

That evening, Maude directed Max to speak to Prince. "Prince," Max began, "cats are not like us. They allow food to remain in their bowls for consumption later. You need to leave it alone."

"But Max," Prince replied, "we know that food left uneaten at meal time is an insult to our owners. Moreover, no food should be left uncovered outside the refrigerator."

Max exercised his alpha-status. "I'm sorry, Prince, this is not negotiable. Leave Maude's food alone."

The next day Max was scheduled for "the works"—clipping, shampoo and air-drying at Pretty Pets, Inc. Sharon asked Prince if he too would like to receive a beauty treatment. Prince frowned, barked and retreated into the living room. Did she think he was a sissy?

Prince chuckled. "Wait until the Polk Park Pack hears about this. Our leader goes in for the full beauty treatment at Pretty Pets."

Max was unfazed. "You know, Prince, a little treatment at Pretty Pets might do you some good. How's your love life lately?"

"Actually," stammered Prince, "I seem to have hit a dry spell."

"Well, there's nothing like a shampoo to increase your sex appeal. Why just last week . . . " Max's voice trailed off as he allowed nostalgia to take over.

"Why don't you come along with me?. You have nothing to lose."

"Thanks, but the grooming scene is not for me. I think I will stay at home with Maude. She has promised to tell me about several successful encounters with chipmunks."

When Max returned, he did not smell like Max. "Egad, Max," Prince said, "how long before the perfume wears off? We should check in at the park tomorrow."

"Not to worry. I'm not concerned about appearing before members of the Polk Park Pack. And, if they know what's good for them, I will be treated with the usual respect."

Meanwhile, Sharon was engaged in a bit of housecleaning. She pushed the sofa back against the wall. She had moved it forward to increase the reach of her vacuum cleaner. Unnoticed by Sharon, however, when she pushed the sofa back, she trapped Maude's cloth mouse. It was imprisoned between a back leg and the wall. Sharon left for her office.

Maude was distraught. Repeated attempts to liberate the mouse by applications of her right paw had failed. She tried to close her jaws on the mouse, but the sofa leg was in the way. Frustrated, she began to whimper.

Prince noticed her distress. "What's wrong?" he asked.

"It's Squeaky," she replied, "he's caught behind the leg of the sofa. I was hoping to play with him."

"I'll get him for you," Prince said. He tried to place his paw between the sofa leg and the wall. There was not enough room.

"Hmm," Prince thought, "this situation requires strategy. Max is very good at strategy. What would he do?"

It seemed to Maude that Prince had developed some form of paralysis. Could it be that he was thinking? Eventually, Prince moved to the front of the sofa. He hooked his right foreleg behind the front leg of the sofa and pulled. No movement. He tried again. Nothing. "I need more leverage," he thought.

Sharon had left a broom in the corner of the kitchen. Prince gripped its handle between his jaws. He dragged the broom into the living room. After a long period of trial and error, he succeeded in wedging the broom handle between sofa leg and wall. It rested on top of Squeaky. Prince then closed his jaws on the business end of the broom, dug in his back heels, and pulled. Success. The sofa moved an inch. Prince removed the broom.

Maude leaped in to retrieve Squeaky. "Prince, you are the best. Thank you," she said. To herself she said, "who could imagine that such a one-dimensional creature would know how to use the mechanical advantage provided by a lever?"

Mutiny at Polk Park

Prince entered the backyard. He barked to announce his presence. Max emerged through the pet flap. "What's up, Prince?" he asked.

"I have bad news, Max. Zeno has taken over leadership of the Polk Park Pack."

"Zeno?" Max replied. "That self-absorbed Labrador-shepherd mix couldn't even lead the pack across the park. He would reason that before he could reach the far side of the park he first would have to go halfway. But to reach the halfway point, he first would have to traverse one-half that distance. And so on. Zeno would conclude that he never even could get started on the journey. A leader who is a prisoner of his own 'logic' is no leader at all."

"Max, you lost me there. It seems to me that Zeno is right. And yet I remember running from one side of the park to the other just yesterday. My head hurts."

"I'll give you a hint. Zeno fails to distinguish two meanings of 'infinite.' There is 'infinite with respect to extendedness' and 'infinite with respect to divisibility.' But let's get back to the problem of leadership. We need to go to the park to confront Zeno."

They met Zeno and the rest of the pack in the playground area of the park. "Zeno, I hear you have taken over leadership of the pack," Max said, while stretching to increase his height.

"Let me explain," Zeno said apologetically. "We have the greatest respect for your leadership. You have made the park safe by chasing out bad people and ill-mannered dogs. But you have other, and more important, responsibilities. We all praise the work you do for Homeland Security. No dog has a better nose. But weekends are when the services of the Polk Park Pack are most needed, and you are not available. That is why we decided that new leadership is needed."

There was a pause. All eyes were on Max. " OK, Zeno, you have a point. I do have other obligations. If the pack feels that this interferes too much with my pack duties, I will step down." Max stopped to gauge the reactions of pack members. Prince, Ralph, Andy, Spot and Dribbler all were looking down at their front paws.

"So be it," said Max. "I leave you in Zeno's paws. Good luck." He turned and headed slowly for the park exit nearest to home.

Back at the park, Zeno and the pack became aware of unusual activity at the playground area. A large kid, Mickey Meehan, interacted with a series of smaller kids. Each encounter featured an exchange of something followed by crying. Mickey was the recipient. The younger kids were the ones in distress.

Prince urged Zeno to take action against the bully. Zeno surveyed the action. "This is some new game the kids have invented." he concluded. "In most games that kids play there are winners and losers. As a rule the biggest and strongest kid wins. This is the natural order of things. I don't think the pack should intervene to disrupt the natural order. *Que sera, sera*, he added, hoping to sound sophisticated.

Andy and Dribbler were not pleased with Zeno's decision, but they concluded that the new leader should be cut some slack. After all, Zeno had no previous executive experience. It might take some time for him to grow into the job.

Things were about to get worse. Mayor Harriet Young arrived at the park with her snow-white Bichon Frisé. Harriet eased her considerable bulk onto a park bench. Angel, the Bichon Frisé, was allowed the run of the park. She immediately accelerated toward the pack. "Good morning, fellow canines, what's happening?" she began. "My name is Angel. My owner is the mayor of this town. I placed second at the Onionville Kennel Club dog show. My presence will enhance the overall appearance of this group. Perhaps if I were to take up a position closer to the front, the pack would not look so seedy."

Sensing a threat to pack identity, Zeno led the pack to the bench that Harriet now shared with a prominent supporter. Taking up a position before the bench, Zeno led a chorus of barks. He hoped that the mayor would take the barking as a protest against Angel's invasion of the pack.

Harriet failed to discern the intent of the barking. She placed her hands over her ears and shouted back at the pack. Zeno concluded that this loud-mouthed woman was too stupid to get their message. He led the pack away. Angel placed herself in the middle of the retreating pack. Harriet reconsidered her evaluation of the situation. "Perhaps those dogs were trying to thank me for allowing Angel to play with them," she said to her companion.

"I'll bet that was it," was the reply.

Patrolman Sloane recently had ridden his chestnut mare Molly along the south edge of the park. Patrols of the park were frequent, but a patrol on horseback was unusual. Molly, without breaking stride, had left a pungent deposit en route to the southeast exit.

Prince pointed out this transgression to Zeno. "This is inappropriate behavior," said Zeno. "On the other hand . . . " Angel had moved to the outside of the pack. She was entertaining the pack with stories about her triumphs in various show competitions. This was an area of experience of no interest to pack members. As Angel drew alongside Molly's unwanted contribution to the landscape, Zeno circled around and shoved her into the pile. Angel struggled to get to her paws. This had the effect of spreading the offensive material over a greater area of her body. The snow-white fur peeked out only at widely spaced intervals.

A downcast Angel returned to her mistress. Harriet was appalled. "Heads will roll," she said to her benchmate. She activated her cell phone and gave instructions to demote Officer Sloane to foot patrol. She added that henceforth there was to be severe disciplinary punishment for any officer that took Molly on patrol without her collection sack. As for that dreadful group of mutts that defiled poor Angel, patrols of the park would be doubled, and pack members would be introduced to Mace.

Several days later, Prince led the pack to the Smith-Grabowski residence. Prince barked three times. Max joined the group in the backyard. Zeno recounted the sagas of Mickey, Molly and Angel. "I am not fit to be alpha-dog," he said sadly. "In each case I led the pack in the wrong direction. Max, we need you to take charge of the pack once again."

Max thought about it for a moment. "Zeno," Max said, "don't give up so easily. You made a couple of decisions that went sour. But those decisions were reasonable in the circumstances. You have run into a string of bad luck, that's all. You need to persevere. You have leadership potential and I will support you whenever I can get to the park." Zeno barked twice in gratitude, and led the pack back to the park.

Maude Reorganizes Sleeping Arrangements

Maude crouched to generate momentum, leaped onto the kitchen countertop, and knocked over the Milk-Bone box. "Sweeten your dog's breath" was written on the side of the box. Maude pried open the top of the box and dislodged a Milk-Bone.

"Max, would you like a Milk-Bone?" she asked.

"Of course, thanks," was the reply.

"It's on one condition Max. You have to grind it up with your teeth for 10 seconds before swallowing."

"That's fine, Maude. I can do that."

"Here it comes," Maude said, as she struck the bone with her paw. It flew off the countertop. Max was on it instantly—another successful display of his catching prowess. He clamped down on it, but then remembered his promise to grind it into powder in his mouth. "This is not natural," he thought, "but it still tastes delicious."

Milk-Bone consumption was part of Maude's plan to regain access at night to the Emily-Sharon bedroom. Sharon recently had declared that the bedroom she shared with Emily was off-limits to four-legged family members. Maude came to the obvious conclusion. The problem was "dog breath." To alleviate it she had devised a plan to improve Max's oral hygiene.

Maude curled up on Emily's lap during the evening ritual of watching the talking box. At 10 o'clock Emily removed Maude, stood up and stretched. Maude took this as a signal that bedtime was imminent. She scampered into the kitchen, intent on liberating another Milk-Bone for Max. If the charm offensive was to succeed, Max's breath had to be at its best. Unfortunately, the Milk-Bone box had been tightly sealed. "What can I do?" Maude pondered. "I have it." She began to howl.

Sharon sensed that Maude was in distress. She entered the kitchen only to find Maude on the counter pawing at the Milk-Bone box. "Emily," said Sharon, " come see what Maude is up to." When Emily arrived, Sharon pointed out that Maude was trying to provide a

Milk-Bone for her buddy Max. Maude was unable to open the box. Hence, the howls of frustration.

"Oh, isn't that adorable," said Emily. Sharon removed a Milk-Bone from the box and placed it where Maude could bat it to the floor. Of course it never hit the floor. Max was too quick. Crunching sounds followed.

"Everything is going well," Maude thought. Sharon and Emily headed upstairs. Maude and Max followed. Upon reaching the closed door to the bedroom Emily gave instructions to Max and Maude. They were to return to their respective beds in the kitchen. Sharon closed the bedroom door.

Maude remained outside the door for a while, whimpering softly. "What's the matter, Maude?" Max asked, "we have comfortable beds of our own downstairs."

"I know Max, but it doesn't compare to Emily-and-Sharon's bed. When I am between them, there is blanket beneath and on both sides of me. It is incredible."

"Come here. Exhale," Maude demanded. "Hmm, that's not too bad. I am beginning to think that our exclusion has nothing to do with the quality of your breath." Maude was correct. The new bedroom policy was based on the discovery of a copious amount of hair shed in the room. Max was the primary culprit. However, there were cat hairs present as well.

Maude realized that a new strategy was required. "Perhaps I could gain access to the bedroom at night if it became clear to Emily and Sharon that only I would be there. I need to convince Max to show no interest in sleeping upstairs. Perhaps I could convince him that his role as head of household security requires his presence on the first floor at night.

"You know, Max," Maude said, "I heard Emily tell Sharon that she feels really secure at night knowing that you are on guard downstairs. Emily and Sharon rely on your keen senses of smell and hearing. And your bark is far more intimidating than any alarm bell."

Max appeared to buy it. Maude's picture of "Max-the-Protector" coincided with his own self-image. "You are right," he said, "the house is safer at night with me downstairs."

Max did not reveal to Maude his second reason for remaining downstairs at night. "When Maude and I sleep upstairs, she establishes a position high up on the bed. There is no room for me there, so I wind up at the foot of the bed. That is OK at first, but at some time during the night, I get kicked by either Emily or Sharon. So I actually prefer to sleep in my comfortable bed downstairs. Kudos, L. L. Bean (or is it Eddie Bauer)?"

Up a Tree

Max and Prince had passed an uneventful hour at Polk Park. As they approached the Smith-Grabowski residence, they heard cries of anguish. Breaking into a trot, they entered the backyard. The cries were coming from the yard's single maple tree. Their source was Maude. She was clinging for her life to a branch some 15 feet above the ground.

"Maude, that's not your usual place for a mid-afternoon nap," Max said.

"Don't make jokes," Maude replied. "I'm terrified up here. Climbing up was a breeze. But I can't climb back down. The thought of moving headfirst down the trunk makes me wheezy. I don't know where I am in my sequence of nine lives. I would land on my paws if I jumped. But I am so high up. I would risk serious injury if I did jump."

Max sought to calm her. "It's OK, we are here now. Just try to relax. You have found a strong branch. Why did you decide to do the cats' version of mountain-climbing anyway?"

"It's one of your species that is responsible," Maude said. "A dog I had not seen before came into the yard. He growled menacingly. He came between me and the pet flap. I climbed the tree to get away from him. He remained at the base of the tree for a time, but finally moved off. Now I'm stuck up here. I really am frightened."

Max looked around the yard for inspiration. He noticed the hammock on the far side of the tree. Emily usually rolled up the mesh after a nap or outdoor reading session. However, she had neglected to do so. The hammock was ready for use, its mesh cover supported at each end at the top of Y-shaped metal rods.

"Prince, do you think we could push that hammock around so that it's under the branch supporting Maude?"

"Let's give it a try," Prince responded. The two dogs applied their shoulders to the near end of the hammock. When they pushed, the far end of the hammock dug into the ground. There was no movement.

"This isn't working," Max said. "You stay here. I will go to the front end and push there. OK, now push hard." There was slow movement. Soon Max and Prince had succeeded in locating the hammock beneath Maude's branch.

"Maude, you can jump down now," Max advised.

"Max, I really appreciate your effort. You too, Prince. But I can't jump onto a mesh like that. I would break my paws."

"Hold on," Max said. "Emily places a soft pillow beneath her head when she is on the hammock. I remember seeing it on the bench in the garage." Max ran to the side door of the garage.

Fortunately, it had been left ajar. Max nudged it open with his nose. The pillow was on the bench as he had remembered. However, it had been placed in a large plastic bag to keep off dust. Max grasped the open end of the bag between his teeth and dragged it to the hammock.

"Prince," Max instructed, "clamp down on the closed end of the plastic bag while I pull out the pillow." This operation was successful. "Now we have to get the pillow onto the hammock," Max said. "Prince, you grasp that end of the pillow. Together we will swing it up and down. When I say 'now', release your end and it will fly onto the hammock." Prince did as instructed. "Now!" Max said. Prince swung his end. Max, however, dropped his end in the process of barking "now!". The pillow remained on the ground.

Max stared at the pillow. "How are we going to get it into the hammock?" he asked. Had she not been in a state of terror, Maude would have been shaking with laughter.

"Look guys," she suggested, "suppose you each grasp one end of the pillow. I will give three 'meows'. On the third 'meow' swing the pillow up onto the hammock."

Max and Prince executed the plan perfectly. "Maude, you are a genius," declared Max, "now jump!"

Maude looked down. It still was a long distance down to the hammock. On the other hand, there now was a fluffy white pillow on which to land. The pillow was directly beneath her. Max and Prince had done a superb job. Maude crouched and said goodbye to the tree branch. It seemed to her that the flight down took a long time. The landing was accomplished successfully, however. "If you have to jump from a tree, try to land on a pillow supported by a hammock," she thought.

Maude lavished praise on Max and Prince. "You are my heroes," she said. "There is nothing you cannot accomplish. I shall refer to you as my 'can-do duo.'" Prince smiled and trotted off for home. He was proud to have played a role in the "rescue Maude" mission.

Max's mood turned dark as he recalled the incident that led to Maude's tree-climbing escape. He left several markers along the edge of the yard to warn trespassers of the carnage to be visited on intruders.

Emily and Sharon returned home from work at the same time. Glancing out the kitchen window, Emily noticed certain changes in the yard. "That's not where I left the hammock," she thought. "And I am sure that I stored the pillow in the garage."

"Sharon, come look at this," Emily said. "Look at the hammock and pillow under the maple. Have we been invaded? Somebody or something has moved the hammock and brought the pillow to it from the garage."

"You're right," Sharon said, "Perhaps the animals decided to play on it. Or maybe you just forgot to return those items to their storage locations last night?"

Neither Emily nor Sharon noticed the glances exchanged by Max and Maude.

Max the Diagnostician

Max entered the kitchen. He headed for his food bowl. He had followed Maude's suggestion to leave a bit of food in his bowl for a mid-morning snack. "Maude really does give good advice," he thought. "I'm hungry now. But I don't have to wait until the evening meal." Max peered down at his bowl. It was empty. "Am I losing my memory?" he asked himself. "I distinctly remember leaving some Kibbles n' Bits for later consumption."

"Maude," he demanded, "did you watch me eat breakfast?"

"Sorry," she replied, "I was upstairs self-grooming. I did hear slurping at your water bowl, however. Do you realize that you slurp water three tongue-laps at a time? It's very rhythmical. But it quickly becomes annoying. Could you perhaps vary the cadence a bit?"

"OK, I'll do that," Max said, trying to hide his suspicion. It seemed to him that there were two possibilities here. Either he had wolfed down his entire breakfast, contrary to his recollection, or some other household member had eaten what he had left. Just in case the latter possibility had been realized, he resolved to track Maude's movements the next day.

Max's deliberations were interrupted by a familiar bark from the Smith-Grabowski backyard. It was Prince. He had Andy with him. Andy was limping badly. "Max will know what to do," Prince thought.

Max noticed immediately that Andy's aroma signature had changed. There was an unpleasant odor that appeared to emanate from Andy's left front paw. Max thought for a moment. "Where have I encountered that odor before? I know. It was at Sacred Heart Hospital. Sharon's Aunt Ruth had been a patient there. Sharon had brought me there to visit her. Patients enjoy petting me. I accept it. It's the least I can do for my human friends." On the way home, Sharon had been talking on her cell phone. The term 'cancer' had occurred frequently. "Is that the name for what I smelled?" Max wondered.

Maude came through the pet flap. Andy growled at her. Prince quickly set him straight. "Maude is a trusted friend," he admonished. Andy limped off. He could not accept the idea of "cat-as-friend." Prince followed him. Max barked "goodbye," promising to think about Andy's problem.

Back in the kitchen, Max conferred with Maude. "How can we help Andy?" he asked. Maude grunted. She was not a fan of canine cat-haters. "Why should I care if that bigot has a sore foot?" she asked.

"Don't be so quick to judge," Max retorted. "Andy's really sick. He is continually in pain. Normally, he has the sunny disposition possessed by nearly all golden retrievers."

"Well," said Maude, "the best thing you can do for Andy is to arrange for him to be examined by a doctor, a dog doctor, of course."

"That's good, Maude. But how can I do that?" Max asked. "Think," Maude said, "doesn't Prince complain that his master is never home?"

"Yes. That's true, " Max replied, "Prince had to wait for dinner until after sundown several days last week."

"And why was that?" Maude asked.

"Oh, I see. Good point Maude. Mrs. Andrews is away and Dr. Andrews works long hours at Millwood Animal Hospital. I remember that now. He removed a splinter from my paw last year. I hated wearing a bandage and that awful neck collar."

Early the next morning, Max trotted to Andy's house. He then walked slowly with Andy to Prince's house. Max barked to alert Prince to their presence. The back door opened. Prince emerged. The door closed behind him.

Max explained to Prince that it was important that his master notice Andy's condition. Prince agreed to participate. The three dogs engaged in a "who can bark the loudest" competition.

Dr. Andrews came out to quell the noise. The neighbors had complained more than once about early-morning barking. Andy started to limp away. Max and Prince turned to look at him. They produced pitiable whining noises. Dr. Andrews responded at once. He approached Andy, bent over, and sniffed his paw. "Andy, old friend," he said, " you may have a squamous cell carcinoma there beneath your nail bed. We need to deal with that."

This diagnosis meant nothing to the dogs. They were pleased with subsequent developments, however. Dr. Andrews took them inside for biscuits. He placed a telephone call to Andy's owner. After some discussion, Dr. Andrews attached a leash and took Andy to his car. He explained to Max and Prince that they were headed for Millwood Animal Hospital. He assured them that the cancerous growth would be removed surgically, and that Andy soon would be back running with the pack. Max and Prince were reassured by the tone of his voice. They barked to show their appreciation as Dr. Andrews drove off.

Rose Leaves Frank

There was a time when male eyes would turn as Rose walked by. That time was in the past. Nevertheless, Rose remained confident of Frank's continuing attention. Her confidence was misplaced. One day, Frank, owner of Grabowski Motors, noticed a potential car buyer in the sales room. All salespersons were otherwise occupied. Frank approached the customer. Cheryl was a mid-thirties divorcee with a swimmer's body and a captivating smile. Frank was instantly smitten. The demonstration car drive was followed by trips to nearby restaurants, and eventually by visits to area motels. Frank was on cloud nine.

Rose became suspicious. Frank's work at Grabowski Motors demanded increasingly long blocks of time. He had developed a war-weary posture at home. He seldom spoke to her.

Rose decided to investigate. She began a late-afternoon surveillance of Grabowski Motors. When Frank left the building at 6 p.m., Rose followed at a discreet distance. Frank collected Cheryl at her apartment. He drove to Carmelo's Ristorante. An hour later, the couple relocated to the Bide-A-While Motel.

The next morning Frank confessed. "I love Cheryl," he declared. Rose was not sympathetic. She no longer saw a ruggedly handsome ex-linebacker. He had been replaced by a shifty-eyed, flabby, high pressure car salesman. "I have to get out of this place," she thought. "I'll call Sharon." Sharon conferred with Emily. They agreed to provide a temporary change of locale for Rose. They began at once to reconfigure the second floor—separate bedrooms for Sharon and Emily and a guest room for Rose.

Max and Maude were appalled by this development. They entertained various strategies to send Rose packing. Max suggested they resume the "charm offensive" that had been successful on a prior visit.*

"I don't think charm will work this time," said Maude. "Rose is looking for support and affection. She most likely would find our attention soothing. We need a new strategy."

On her first night in residence, Rose returned from the upstairs bathroom to the study-turned-guest-bedroom. She was barefoot. She moved along the length of the bed, preparing to turn off the lamp on the bedside table. Her right foot just missed the dead mouse that Maude had placed there. Rose shrieked and jumped onto the bed. Sharon was quickly on the scene. "I'm so sorry, Mom," she said. "Maude was so pleased to see you that she brought you a present. There is no higher tribute from a cat."

Rose was anything but appreciative. "A dead mouse," she screamed, "She brought me a dead mouse!" It took a few minutes for Rose to calm down. She tossed and turned the entire night.

On her second night in residence, Rose heard scratching noises on her door. She arose to determine its source. Maude had fled down the stairs. Rose descended to the kitchen. There she discovered Max and Maude sleeping peacefully in their pet beds. Rose returned to bed. Soon there was more scratching. Rose placed a pillow over her head in an unsuccessful attempt to block the noise.

At breakfast the next morning, Maude and Max greeted Rose with enthusiasm. Rose did not respond. Maude whispered to Max, "It's your turn today."

Emily and Sharon left for work, leaving Rose nominally in charge of the household. She was on her third cup of coffee when Max slipped his leash off its hook and dropped it on Rose's lap. At first, Rose was annoyed, but then she decided that a walk in the brisk morning air might do her good. She grabbed a "Mutt Mitt" from the package by the back door and allowed Max to lead her through the yard onto the sidewalk beyond.

Max stopped at the first tree between sidewalk and road. He started to sit, stopped halfway, and unloaded. Rose reluctantly applied the "Mutt Mitt." They proceeded toward the park. Three trees along, Max stopped again. The process was repeated. Rose already had used the "Mutt Mitt." She looked around to see if anyone was watching, and then moved away from the scene of the crime. She was aware of looks of condemnation from pedestrians heading toward her.

At the park, she released Max to join Zeno, Prince and Spot. She was tired after just a quarter-mile walk. There were dog-waste bags in a container on a post nearby. She debated taking one back to clean up Max's excess. "I'll do that on the way back," she resolved.

Rose started to nod off, despite the unforgiving surface of the park bench. Max arrived with Zeno, Prince and Spot. They all were thirsty. No one in the park had brought water for the resident dog population. Max nudged Rose. He grabbed his leash, indicating his desire to return home. Rose obliged. "Perhaps I will be able to sneak in a nap," she thought.

Rose did not expect to be leading the entire pack. Max walked along beside her. He was on best behavior. The other three members of the pack trailed behind, hoping that Max would provide a much-needed drink.

Back home, Rose disappeared into the kitchen. She returned quickly with four plastic bowls, a box of dog biscuits, and a pitcher of water. The pack members gratefully hydrated. They were surprised and delighted when Rose then distributed biscuits. The pack, minus Max, trotted off, having formed a positive opinion of houseguest Rose.

Rose opted for an early bedtime that evening. Emily and Sharon shared impressions of her visit. "She's been amazing," Emily said, "she does the shopping, prepares dinner, and even takes Max for walks."

"I'm glad you feel that way," Sharon replied. "What has impressed me is the total absence of complaints about the lack of men in my life."

Max and Maude overheard this exchange. Max looked at Maude and said "perhaps we have been too hard on Rose. She keeps our water bowls full and she is generous with pet treats. Moreover, she is well-regarded by members of the Polk Park Pack. I say let's abandon our plans to drive her away."

"Agreed," said Maude.

Rose's cell phone rang as she was preparing for a good night's sleep. She wondered if it was Frank on the line. It was not. Sister Frances wanted to know if Rose would housesit for a month while she and husband Karl vacationed in Europe. Rose accepted the offer at once.

A Visit from Rose Grabowski.

Not on Our Watch

"I'm bored, Maude," Max declared. "Emily and Sharon are at work, Prince is on vacation with his owners, and you've been asleep."

"I'm awake now, thank you very much." Maude replied, "what do you want to do? How about a game of hide-and-seek?"

"Sure, why not," Max said. "I'll stay here in the kitchen until the long pointer on the clock is vertical."

Maude headed upstairs. "Dogs are ground-bound creatures," she recalled. "I'll just leap to the top of this wardrobe. It will never occur to Max to look up."

Maude was correct. Max entered the guest room. He looked beneath the bed and at other hiding places on the floor. Maude snickered as he left the room. Max heard her. He looked up and spotted her. "There you are. Very sneaky."

Max and Maude returned to the kitchen. Max enjoyed a drink. "I think I will head for the park," he announced. "Without Prince to keep him grounded, Zeno is likely to lead the pack into trouble."

Max was prescient. Pierre Rideaux, an accomplished pickpocket, had befriended the pack. Pierre recognized Zeno's status as alpha-dog. He called him over to his location on a park bench. Pierre withdrew four plastic bowls from his backpack and filled them with water. The four dogs gratefully lapped up the liquid. Pierre singled out Zeno for a dog biscuit. It was consumed quickly. He then provided biscuits for the other three dogs. There was general approval of this newcomer to the park.

As Max entered the park, he noticed a minor collision on the north-south path. No damage was done. Pierre apologized effusively for his clumsiness. Unnoticed by his victim, Pierre had liberated his wallet. "This was no ordinary transaction," Max thought, "there was no exchange of wallet for something else. The man who engineered the collision removed the other's wallet without his knowledge."

Max alerted Zeno to the theft. "Pierre wouldn't do something like that," Zeno said, "he is a great guy. He brings us water and biscuits."

Max knew what he had seen. He was disappointed by Zeno's reaction. Max decided to follow Pierre as he left the park. Pierre entered an alley on his right. He stopped to remove cash and credit cards from the wallet. He then tossed the empty wallet into a garbage can. He gave no thought to the dog at the entrance to the alley. The dog was seated, scratching his right ear.

Pierre entered a nearby car and drove off. Max returned to the park. He had planned to have a serious discussion with Zeno about that thief Pierre. He decided to postpone that discussion, however, when he saw Officer Charlie Oliver, his sometime airport-security partner. Oliver's shift had just ended, and he'd entered the park on his way home. Max barked a greeting. He accepted the expected behind-the-ears scratching.

Max began his "I have discovered something" barking routine. Oliver was puzzled by this display. There were no people or packages nearby. Max tugged on his pants leg, indicating that Oliver was to follow. Oliver decided to give Max the benefit of the doubt. Max had never failed to produce. He followed Max to the garbage can where Pierre had thrown the empty wallet. Oliver lifted the cover and peered inside. "Sorry Max, it's empty." he reported.

Max was confused. A few minutes earlier it had been full with the wallet on top.

That evening, Max expressed his frustration to Maude. "Well, Max," she said, "It looks like there is more work to be done by Detective Dog. Better take your cap, pipe, and magnifying glass to the park tomorrow."

Max arrived early. "Zeno," he counseled, "keep an open mind about this Pierre person. He stole a man's wallet yesterday." Zeno nodded, but clearly was unconvinced.

Joan Branch, one of Zeno's favorite people, arrived at the park, carrying a shoulder bag and leading a toddler. She and Jamie, aged four, took over a park bench. Zeno approached. He allowed Jamie to maul him. Joan provided the anticipated reward—a liver treat. Zeno's tail wagged furiously. Jamie reached for it, but Zeno was too quick. He turned away to rejoin Max. The two dogs joined the other members of the pack at the far end of the park.

Joan was absorbed by activities on her cell phone as Jamie "went walkies." She looked up in time to see him near the sidewalk at the park's edge. "Jamie," she called, as she entered pursuit mode.

Pierre swooped in to occupy the recently vacated bench. He was drawn to the bench by the shoulder bag Joan had left while she sought to corral her toddler. Pierre unfolded his newspaper to full length, slid Joan's bag behind it, and removed its wallet. That accomplished, he refolded the paper, stretched, and casually strolled toward a park exit.

Zeno had been watching Pierre as he conversed with Max. He noticed that Joan's shoulder bag had been moved toward the center of the bench. Meanwhile, Pierre was moving away.

"Let me handle this," Zeno said, "Pierre and I have a good relationship." Pierre spotted Zeno's approach and stopped. Zeno wagged his tail and looked up expectantly. "All right, Zeno, let's see what we can find." Pierre shrugged out of his backpack, placed it on the ground, unzipped it, and found a biscuit for Zeno.

While Pierre was distracted, Max swooped by, grasped the backpack by its straps, and dragged it toward the park exit. Pierre, outraged, called out "come back here, you mutt." He began to pursue Max. Zeno, however, had mobilized the pack. They surrounded Pierre before he could get up to speed. Ralph tripped him. When he sought to rise, Zeno and Spot jumped on him. It took some time before Pierre could extricate himself.

Meanwhile, Max had made slow but steady progress down the sidewalk outside the park. He reached the front door of the Millwood Police Station, released the backpack and barked loudly. Officer Oliver emerged. Pierre changed his mind about pursuit, executed a U-turn, and retreated back toward the park.

Charlie Oliver invited Max into the Station for water and a biscuit. He spread the contents of the backpack on a table. The woman's wallet was out of place among dog treats, a set of lock picks, a false mustache, and the latest edition of *Playboy*. Charlie sent the wallet off for fingerprint analysis.

The Cat on His Back Knows Naught About That

"Stay tuned for 'Uncle Ike's Menagerie', coming to you after these messages," pleaded the announcer. The messages turned out to be aimed at individuals with beer bellies, wrinkled skin, or erectile dysfunction. Sharon observed that there were a number of men in her office who aced this trifecta. Emily smiled and placed her arm around Sharon.

This action destroyed Maude's snooze-state. The TV screen claimed her attention. Uncle Ike was at its center. On his right were a boxer and a standard poodle. On his left were a Siamese, a Persian and a British shorthair. "It's about time cats received some airtime on TV," Maude declared. The cats on screen were members of Uncle Ike's stable of performing animals. The program featured cats jumping through hoops, cats scrambling to stay on top of large balls, and cats riding dogs as if they were jockeys on horses.

"Max," Maude said, "do you think we could perform some of those acts? Perhaps we could put together a show for Emily and Sharon."

"I don't see why not," Max replied, "we could practice on the beach ball in the basement. Do you remember Emily and Sharon playing with it at the beach last summer?"

"I do remember," Maude said. "Sharon and Emily exchanged tosses. Sharon invariably caught Emily's tosses, even when they were off target. Emily sometimes managed to catch Sharon's return throws, each of which was directly to her."

Several males had gathered to watch the (partial) display of athletic ability. Onlookers were heard to mumble, "What a waste" and "I bet I could straighten them out."

The session in the basement did not go well. Every time Max tried to mount the beach ball his approach was slightly off-center and he fell off to the side. Maude did not fare better. Only once did she manage to reach the top of the ball. Once there, she was unable to do anything except slide off to the floor.

"This is harder than it looked on TV," Max concluded. "Our beach-ball technique is poor. However, I'll bet we could do the 'jockey-on-a-horse' routine."

"OK, I'll give it a try," Maude said. "Hold still and pay no attention to my claws."

Maude landed on Max's back on the first try. Max winced and then made a slow circuit of the basement. "Maude, I think we have it," he said with more than a hint of satisfaction. "What we need is a routine that will impress our audience. Let me think for a moment."

"Perhaps we could use one of Uncle Ike's routines," Maude suggested. "Do you remember the one where the cat-on-dog approached a tunnel? The cat jumped off. The dog proceeded through the tunnel. The cat ran on top of the tunnel and leaped back onto the dog at the other end."

"That's good. Emily and Sharon will be impressed," Max replied. "But wait a minute, we don't have a tunnel."

"We could pretend that the kitchen table is a tunnel," Maude said. "You would have to nudge the chairs away from the table to create a path beneath. The table height should not be a problem. I can easily leap from your back onto the tabletop and leap back down onto your back at the far end."

"Good plan, Maude," Max replied. "Let's give it a try."

Max pushed back the chairs. He gathered Maude and slowly approached the table. Maude leaped up, strolled to the far end of the table, and reattached to Max. It was a perfect dress rehearsal. It remained to assemble an audience.

After dinner, family members occupied their usual viewing positions in front of the TV. Max sensed that the screen now featured a commercial. He signaled Maude. Maude dutifully leaped onto Max's back. Max circled the room. Having gained the attention of Emily and Sharon, he entered the kitchen. Maude dismounted. Max adjusted the chairs.

Max barked to call attention to the act. Emily and Sharon were attentive. Maude hopped on. The two animals executed perfectly the "under- and-over-the-table" routine.

There was sustained applause from Emily and Sharon. Max and Maude beamed. Max took the applause to be a demand for an encore. He circled around to pass again under the table. His motion was accompanied by another example of perfect timing from Maude.

Just after she landed again on Max's back, there was a bark produced in the back yard. Max processed it. "That was not a bark delivered by any of my friends. There is an intruder in the back yard." Max was through the pet flap in a flash. He issued three barks, prefaced and finished with a growl. The intruder looked up and elected to flee. Max observed his flight. "This is a satisfactory result," he thought. However, he had a nagging feeling that all was not well.

Max reentered the kitchen. There, to the side of the pet flap was an unconscious Maude. Maude had managed to turn sideways as Max exited through the flap. Her left shoulder absorbed most of the impact. However, she also struck her head on the kitchen door.

Maude commenced to moan. Emily gathered her up in her arms. Sharon preceded her to the car. Max pleaded to be included. Sharon consulted with Emily, and then opened the back door of the car for him.

Max was disconsolate. He realized that he was responsible for Maude's injury. He had allowed his instincts to overwhelm him. Max sat on the back seat, whimpering softly, waiting for Emily and Sharon to return from inside the animal hospital.

Forty minutes later, Emily emerged, carrying Maude. Maude had been examined and given a mild tranquilizer. She had a badly bruised shoulder and a concussion. The pet doctor had prescribed medication for pain relief during two days of rest. She assured Sharon and Emily that Maude soon would be back to good health. Maude's woozy understanding of the situation was "that was number four, but I still have five left."

Max did his best to promote Maude's recovery. He allowed her to curl up beside him during her naps. Maude found his body warmth to be comforting, and perhaps restorative.

Maude the Oracle

Max was in lecture mode. "Maude," he declared, "a philosopher—it may have been Yogi Berra or Satchel Paige—once said that 'the unexamined life is not worth living.' As you recover from your encounter with the kitchen door (my fault entirely), it is a good time to reconsider your life goals."

"If I may offer a few observations," Max continued, "1) it is good to rid the house of mice, 2) it is a matter of indifference whether the chipmunk population is reduced, and 3) it is not good to seek to destroy birds, however inept the seeking. The songs of birds are good things to have in the world. Of course, the warblings of birds do not rise to the heights achieved in your singing."

Maude's pained expression told Max that his appraisal was not well-received. Noting this, Max adopted a more positive approach. "Maude," he said, "you excel in the role of affectionate pet. You bring joy to the lives of Emily and Sharon." Max paused, noting an improvement in Maude's expression. He took this improvement to be a signal to continue.

"Five days a week, Emily and Sharon are at work," Max noted. "There is time here for you to realize your true potential. You excel at the analysis and resolution of problems. Why not use some of your 9-to-5 time to help others who are trapped in various life situations? Imagine the aid and comfort you could provide your fellow cats . . . and dogs, too, of course. I foresee Maude Smith-Grabowski of Millwood taking her rightful place among the great oracles of the world: Pythia of Delphi, Warren Buffett of Omaha, and Phil of Punxsutawney."

"I dunno, Max," Maude replied. "How would I know who is in trouble? During my recovery from my time as 'dog-jockey,' I am confined to quarters."

"I will let it be known that your advice is available upon request," Max replied. "I have a network of friends who will spread the word about your insights. I will collect information about problem-situations, inform you about them, and convey back your advice about solutions."

Maude delivered solutions for the first batch of queries:

1) From Cinnamon: "I am a golden retriever. How can I get my owners to leave me at home when they go to the beach? They always insist that I accompany them. I can't stand the hot sand on my paws. I feel that they are about to catch fire."

Reply from Maude the Oracle: "Cinnamon, do your owners put up a beach umbrella during these family outings? If they do, make sure that you stay in its shadow. The sand there will not be as hot. Good luck."

2) From Topsy: "Every time I try to visit the bowl containing cat food, Eva, the other cat in residence, chases me away. I have pleaded with her to share the food, but she is a bully. She attacks me just for kicks. What can I do?"

Reply from Maude the Oracle: "Topsy, when you are hungry, announce that there is a mouse in the cellar. Say that you chased it, but it was too fast for you. When Eva leaves to show you how a mouse is caught, help yourself to the cat food."

3) From Fluffy: "I am forced to live with a drooling Bulldog named Bruno. We share a water bowl. Every time he drinks, he leaves a copious amount of spit. Soon the water is half dog-drool. What can I do?"

Reply from Maude the Oracle: "If your owners leave a bathroom door open, you are in luck. Tell Bruno that the owners have prepared 'special water' for him there. Bruno will quench his thirst in the toilet bowl, leaving the water in the kitchen for you."

Word spread quickly about the helpful advice available from Maude the Oracle. She gracefully accepted thanks from satisfied correspondents. She almost had settled into her new role when she received the following complaint.

4) From Shep: "I am one of three dogs in the Gibson household. Spike has assumed alpha-status. He has established a dictatorship. At mealtime, Terri (the third member of the group) and

I are required to wait until Spike has consumed the food in his bowl before we begin to eat. If he is still hungry after finishing his bowl, he eats his fill from our bowls. Only after he can eat no more are Terri and I permitted to eat. What can I do in this situation?"

Reply from Maude the Oracle: "The only way to end a dictatorship is to confront the bully. The next time Spike takes your food, bite him as hard as you can. He will get the message."

Max reported to Maude the next day that Shep had been taken to the pet hospital with life-threatening wounds. "The Gibsons are very upset. They have sent Spike off to a farm upstate. Meanwhile, Mrs. Gibson has been at the pet hospital nearly continuously."

Maude was very upset to hear this. She had recommended that Shep confront Spike. The result was a tragedy. Maude resolved to shut down the "Maude the Oracle" franchise.

"Max," she said, "I know you meant well. But giving advice at a distance is too risky. From now on I will restrict my recommendations to problem situations for which I have direct personal knowledge."

Pet Parade

Sharon pushed her chair back from the table and crossed her legs. "It's Friday, should we indulge a bit?" she asked Emily. "There is a bit of Bailey's Irish Cream left."

"That sounds good. Let's leave the dishes and adjourn to the living room."

Max and Maude anticipated the move. Maude took up a position on the sofa designed to maximize her comfort when the women arrived. Max sat alongside the sofa ready to catch any snack that might accompany the liqueur.

"The annual pet parade is to be held in Polk Park on Sunday," Emily said. She looked down at Maude and Max. Maude curled up on her lap. Max placed his jaw on her thigh and presented his "I would love a treat" look. "What do you think, Sharon, do we have blue-ribbon candidates here?"

"I don't know. I fear we may be in a 'silk purse from a sow's ear' situation." This allusion was lost on Max and Maude. However, they sensed that there was something non-complimentary about it. Max moved away. He reentered the kitchen to make sure that there was no item of food on the floor that he had missed. Maude stretched out, demanding to be stroked.

"It might be fun to dress them up," Emily conceded. "Does anything suggest itself when you look at them?"

"I see Max as Sherlock Holmes," Sharon said. "We have a plaid dog jacket. We would need a deerstalker cap, a magnifying glass and a pipe. I'm sure we could talk him into wearing the jacket and cap and carrying the magnifying glass around his neck. But I don't know about the pipe. Do you suppose he could be taught to hold it between his teeth?"

"I can visualize that," Emily replied. "I think it's worth a try. But how about Maude? She's more of a ham than Max. She would be most upset not to be given a costume and an opportunity to perform for the judges."

Sharon thought for a moment. " I remember when we moved in here you had a doll dressed as Cinderella. Do you still have it? I could see Maude as Cinderella."

"You may have something there," Emily replied. "The doll should be in the attic crawl space. It came with an open-top carriage. I remember placing Cinderella in the carriage and wheeling her off to the ball. If the Cinderella dress can be altered to fit Maude, we could install Maude in the carriage and pull her past the judges."

Emily retrieved the Cinderella ensemble from the attic. Sharon removed the dress. She placed it against Maude's body as she napped. "I think we can make this work," Sharon said, "I wonder if we could talk Maude into wearing the tiara?"

It turned out that Maude was delighted to prance around the house with the sparking headpiece.

"This parade will be such fun," Emily said. "I'll take Max to the park for a Frisbee session. While there I will register Max and Maude for Sunday's parade. There's a kiosk in the park for that purpose."

On parade day, Max, with Sharon alongside, was fifth in line. Moving past the judges he swiveled his head around. His gaze said "I am not just looking at you, I am *observing* you." It was not clear that the judges were aware of the significance of Holmes' gaze. The tall judge, in particular, seemed to have a negative appraisal of Max's performance.

Maude sat regally in her coach, twenty-first in line. She was unaware that The Baron had infiltrated the crowd of onlookers. "There is that insolent Persian that tried to muscle in on my territory in back of Fletcher's Fish Market," he said to himself.* The Baron was a tomcat of action. He charged Cinderella's carriage, dislodging the left front wheel. As the carriage toppled over, Maude leaped into Emily's arms. Emily kicked out at The Baron, who quickly retreated into the crowd. Maude's parade was over.

The three judges met to evaluate the participants. "I really liked the dog dressed as Sherlock Holmes," said Sally Bane, the youngest of the judges. "Yes, but I thought he ruined the impression by holding the pipe with its bowl facing down," replied Judge Norton. Marie Norton was the principal organizer of the parade. She also provided financial support for the event. The other judges were careful to defer to her judgment about the contestants. Max was not singled out. Instead the judges rewarded the dachshund who impersonated a hot dog.

Maude, of course, was never in the running. To be eligible for an award, a contestant had to complete the parade by passing in front of the judges. The Baron had seen to it that this presentation did not occur.

The following weekend, Fran and Donald Smith were visiting. Emily saw an opportunity for some after-dinner entertainment. She left Fran and Donald in Sharon's care while she dressed Max and Maude for their comeback tour.

This time Max held the pipe with its bowl facing up. Maude was serene as Cinderella, secure in the belief that The Baron was far away. The repaired carriage wheel fell off again, but only after passing the reviewing team of Fran and Donald. The team delivered a chorus of "bravos".

* *Fish a la Cart.*

Dealing with Cheryl

Maude was curled up on Sharon's lap. She drifted off into a dream about the display window at Fletcher's Fish Market. There were gorgeous specimens of salmon, halibut, striped bass, tuna and trout. Maude produced a contented purring sound. This sound was overridden, however, by a persistent buzzing from the left back pocket of Sharon's jeans. Maude's dream ended abruptly as Sharon shifted her hips to gain access to her cell phone. Maude hopped down. She headed for her water bowl in the kitchen.

"That was Frank," Sharon said to Emily, replacing the cell phone. "He asked if he could stop by tomorrow afternoon. There's something he wants to discuss with me."

"I wonder what that could be," Emily said. "Do you suppose he will want to stay overnight? We better rearrange the second floor just in case."

Maude took note of these rearrangements. "Max, what is going on?" she asked, "Did Sharon and Emily have a fight?"

"Not that I know of," he replied. "I did hear something about a visit from Frank."

Frank arrived at 4 p.m. Saturday with Cheryl in tow. Introductions were made. "Pleased ta meetcha," Cheryl said. She clearly was nervous. She attacked her gum with vigor.

Frank took center stage. He commanded the podium. "Cheryl and I have been seeing each other for six weeks now," he declared. "It has been the most exciting time of my life."

"Ooh, Frankie," Cheryl contributed.

"I want you to get to know Cheryl," Frank continued. "She and I plan to get married as soon as my divorce comes through."

"Your divorce!" exclaimed Sharon. "You're planning to divorce Mom?"

"Don't be upset, Sharon. You know that your mother and I have not been getting along lately. Divorce is best for all concerned."

"Dad, are you forgetting that marriage is a sacrament, a lifetime commitment? You must realize that the Church does not recognize divorce."

"I know that. Cheryl and I realize that we will not be able to have a church wedding. This is the unfortunate consequence of my not meeting her first."

Cheryl beamed in response.

There followed a period of awkward silence. Max entered the house following a trip to the backyard. He approached Cheryl. Cheryl recoiled, pushing hard into the sofa back.

"Cheryl is afraid of dogs," Frank offered by way of apology. "She was frightened as a young girl when a pack of barking dogs surrounded her." Max retreated to the kitchen, muttering under his breath that some human beings are an unnecessary drain on the planet's resources.

Maude joined Max in the kitchen for a conference. It was clear to both that Sharon was very upset. Max asked Maude if she had any ideas about a "remove Cheryl" strategy. "I'm afraid not, Max," Maude replied, "every plan I come up with results in a stronger bond between Cheryl and Frank. For example, suppose we were to take advantage of her fear of dogs. You could growl at her and pretend to stalk her, but this only would make Frank more protective of her."

"I could spread Cheryl's underwear on the bathroom floor, or spill her perfume on his suit, but Frank would blame us, or Sharon, rather than Cheryl. I can't think of any way to drive a wedge between Frank and Cheryl," Maude regretfully concluded.

Back in the living room, Frank insisted on taking Sharon and Emily to dinner at Sybil's Steak House. Emily claimed to have a prior engagement. She spent some time at her office, preparing a standard prenuptial agreement. The agreement left blank the names of the participants, the amount of money involved, and its relation to 'years of service.' Sharon had suggested that leaving such a document in a place where Cheryl would discover it might cause her to reassess her relationship with Frank.

At dinner, Sharon volunteered to be 'designated driver' so that Frank and Cheryl could indulge their love affair with the fermented grape. This indulgence turned out to be considerable. Frank was in no condition to drive from the Smith-Grabowski house to his own residence. Sharon prepared the futon for overnight use.

Frank and Cheryl were sleeping it off when Emily returned with the prenuptial agreement. "What should we do with this?' she asked Sharon.

"We should place it where Cheryl, and not Frank, will discover it," Sharon replied.

An opportunity to accomplish this arose the next morning. Frank took Max for a walk. Cheryl was in the upstairs bathroom shower, singing "My Heart Belongs to Daddy." Sharon entered the spare room, opened Frank's briefcase, and placed the prenuptial form inside. She then closed the briefcase so that a corner of the form protruded. The protruding corner seemed to be saying "open this briefcase."

Cheryl fell into Sharon's trap. She opened Frank's briefcase and removed the prenuptial agreement. Her first response was rage. She prepared to confront Frank with a combination of tears and recriminations.

"No, that would not be smart," she said to herself upon reflection. "The best thing to do is replace the form in the briefcase and pretend I have not seen it. I should let Frank be the first to bring up the question about the distribution of our resources—considerable in his case, nonexistent in mine."

Cheryl's strategy was sound. Frank did not discover the prenuptial form until after he and Cheryl had returned home. He was furious. "What's wrong, dear?' Cheryl asked.

"It's nothing," Frank responded. He resolved to deal with Sharon at another time.

Lost in Millwood

Max was processing aromas wafting in from the partially open back window of the squad car, when he heard a disembodied voice. It was the squad-car equivalent of the radio in the Smith-Grabowski kitchen. "All units, reported home invasion at 25 Lakewood Street. Respond please." "Unit Seven responding," said Officer Charlie Oliver. I am alone with sniffer dog Max, but will investigate."

Approaching 25 Lakewood Street, Oliver spotted a man with a loaded garbage bag slung over his shoulder. He was moving rapidly away from the scene of the crime. Oliver stopped the squad car. He jumped out to pursue the robber. The robber had two advantages. He had a 200-yard lead, and knowledge of the neighborhood. He disappeared down a side street, followed shortly thereafter by Oliver.

Max didn't know what to do. Charlie had closed the front door of the car on leaving. Two girl joggers came down the road. Max barked loudly, hoping they would stop and let him out. However, the girls were frightened by the barking. They shifted into high gear, leaving Max imprisoned in the car.

Minutes passed, and then a seven-year-old boy approached the car. Max adopted a different approach. He smiled at the boy with his best "let's play together" look. Jackie Craig scratched his nose, pushed his glasses back, and opened the door to greet Max. Max wagged his tail softly and rubbed against the boy's legs.

Jackie reached down for Max's leash. Max pulled it away as he sped after Oliver and the robber. Unfortunately, his nose received no useful message. No scent that he could trace remained on the road. Max ran along several streets looking for Oliver, but his search was unsuccessful. He tried barking to indicate his presence. There was no response.

Panting freely, Max stopped to take account of his situation. He was in an unfamiliar neighborhood. "I'm lost," he said to himself, "I have no idea how to get home."

A large Rottweiler dozed in the yard of a three-story Victorian mansion on Max's right. At Max's approach, Brutus awakened, snarled and accelerated toward him. Before reaching the sidewalk, Brutus pulled up suddenly, barking at Max all the time. Max was relieved that Brutus was constrained by a sub-yard electric fence. He continued on down the road. A standard poodle in the next block was more friendly. Unfortunately, she had no idea where Polk Park was.

Max continued to look around. A young girl was hosting a tea party in the driveway of her house. She was seated at a card table with a stuffed bear and an oversized mouse. Max approached cautiously. Amy looked up, pointed to the vacant place at the table, and invited Max to "sit." He did so.

Amy did not have tea in the pot. It was just water. She poured some into the cup placed before the mouse. Max looked at Amy. She moved the cup and saucer to Max's place at the table. Max produced a low bark of appreciation. He was very thirsty. He looked up expectantly. Amy was bright for an eight-year old. She saw the problem. She poured the water from the cup into the saucer. Max consumed it in two tongue laps. Amy then poured water directly from the teapot into the saucer. Max drank it all. He then circled the table to allow Amy to pet his head. Amy was delighted to have made a real friend. Bear and mouse were forgotten.

Kim Schelling arrived home with clothing retrieved from a dry cleaner. Kim moved with the grace of a dancer, long blond hair creating waves in the process. She noticed the addition to Amy's tea party. "Look, Mommy," Amy said, "'Sir Arthur' has come to live with us. He is my very best friend." Kim smiled and turned to look at 'Sir Arthur.' Max offered his right paw. This produced the desired response. "What a sweet dog," Kim said.

"Sweet?" Max thought. "Oh well, I'll take it."

Kim reached out to pet "Sir Arthur." She leaned over to read what was inscribed on his collar. "Amy," she announced, "'Sir Arthur' has another name. People call him 'Max.'"

"'Max', I love it," Amy replied. "Mommy please, may we keep him. We really need a dog."

"Amy dear, Max is part of a family somewhere. There's a telephone number on his collar. Somehow he got lost. We need to contact his owner."

"But I want to keep him," Amy wailed, "He came to our house. He likes it here. See, his tail is wagging."

Kim dialed the number engraved on Max's collar. There was no answer. She left a message about Max. Amy suggested that Max might be hungry. Max barked softly to indicate that food would be appreciated. Kim thought for a moment. "We don't have any dog food," she said. "But I did save the hamburger patty you refused to finish last night. Max might like that."

Max did like it. He wolfed it down and looked up expectantly. "Is that all, one-half a child's portion?" he seemed to ask.

"Let's play hide-and-seek," Amy suggested. "I'll hide first." Amy left the kitchen for her favorite hiding place behind the sofa. She produced a weak whistle to activate the search. Max followed the suppressed giggles to reunite with Amy. Amy responded with a big hug. "Your turn Max," she said. Max had participated in sequences like this before. He knew what to do. He surveyed the living room, choosing a spot behind a stuffed chair.

The telephone rang before Amy could resume the game. Sharon had returned home from work and noticed the telephone-message indicator light blinking. She called Kim to see if Max was OK. Ten minutes later, she arrived at Kim's house. Max barked joyfully, launching himself into Sharon's arms. Sharon staggered backward but recovered, lowering Max to the kitchen floor.

"I can't thank you enough for saving Max," Sharon said. "If you don't have anything planned, please come over to our house. My roommate Emily would like to thank you as well. We could order some pizzas, open some wine and celebrate Max's return."

"Can we, Mommy? I want to see where Max lives," Amy said.

"That's very nice of you," Kim said, flashing a dazzling smile. Amy and I will follow you in our car."

"Can Max ride with us, Mommy?" Amy pleaded. Max's glance told Sharon that this arrangement was acceptable.

After pizza slices (including two for Max), and two bottles of Vino Nobile di Montepulciano, Kim began to weep as she recounted the recent departure of husband Phil. Phil had run off with a coworker who had been transferred to Seattle. It seemed that nine years of marriage had passed down the drain. Kim had put on a brave face for Amy's sake, but the wine, and the sympathetic environment created by Sharon and Emily, led to an unleashing of suppressed emotions.

Meanwhile Amy discovered Maude. She pursued Maude around the house, stroking her fur every time Maude paused. Maude soon realized that Amy was not a tail-puller. She found Amy's attentions to be more than acceptable.

At ten o'clock, not one of the three women could pass a sobriety test. Sharon and Emily invited Kim to occupy the guest room upstairs. Amy was placed on the futon in the study, with the promise that Max and Maude would be free to join her. Shortly thereafter slumber prevailed in all three rooms.

Morning light entered the master bedroom. Emily's first thought was that it was Sunday. Arising was optional. She stretched out, reaching for Sharon. Sharon was not there. Emily pictured Sharon in the kitchen, making coffee, cooking bacon and preparing eggs for scrambling. However, there was no aroma of coffee or bacon. Emily threw on a robe and descended to the kitchen. Max heard her descend. He leaped down from the futon to follow her downstairs.

Sharon, however, was not in the kitchen. A frown came across Emily's face. Evidently Sharon had chosen to comfort Kim at some point during the night. Emily filled Max's bowl. She then returned to the bedroom she normally shared with Sharon. Donning an outfit suitable for jogging, she returned to the kitchen. Max took one look at her and pointed to his leash. He was not disappointed. He enjoyed the morning air as Emily pondered recent developments on the second floor.

Why Not a Trio?

"Maude," Max began, "I sense tension in the Smith-Grabowski household. Have you noticed it?"

"Yes, I am aware that all is not well between Sharon and Emily. I have been thinking about what we could do to improve the situation. The first step is to find out the cause of the recent frosty atmosphere. Any ideas, Max?"

"Well," Max said, after a moment's reflection, "I noticed this morning that Sharon forgot to reset the toaster on 'medium' after she had toasted a frozen bagel. Emily was not pleased. Her toast was burned. I caught her giving Sharon an accusing glance."

"Yes," Sharon's negligence must have been a disappointment to Emily," Maude replied. "But I think there's a deeper problem. Are you aware that Sharon has been sleeping in the guest bedroom? Why do you think she moved out of the master bedroom she shared with Emily?"

"Why, to make more room for us," Max suggested. "You have more room now on Emily's bed and I have more room on the guest-room bed with Sharon. I thought it was very considerate of them to make us more comfortable."

"No, no Max, you're missing the point here," Maude said in desperation. "The change of bed occupancy has nothing to do with us. It has to do with Kim Schelling."

"But Kim's not even here," Max said. "Besides, we all like Kim."

"That's true, Max, "Maude replied, "but Sharon likes Kim too much."

"I don't understand," Max objected, "how can one human being like another too much? I can't imagine a situation in which someone liked me too much."

"Max, think a moment. Remember that when Cheryl arrived on the scene, this made trouble for Frank and Rose Grabowski.*

What happened was that the bond between Frank and Rose was broken and that a new bond between Frank and Cheryl was forged."

"I know that. I was there," Max said. "What has that to do with the bond between Sharon and Emily?"

"Kim is playing the role of Cheryl," Maude explained. "She has come to take Sharon away from Emily."

"I don't understand," Max complained. "It's not as if Kim were a man and Sharon and Emily were competing for him. They are all women. Why can't three women get along, just as well as two?"

Maude thought about that for a while. "I think you have an interesting point there, Max. My instincts say that pairs always emerge within groups of three. Alliances may shift. But there always is that tendency to degenerate into 'two-against-one'. That is the human condition from which there is 'no exit.'"

Maude's lecture was interrupted by loud voices from upstairs. Sharon currently held the floor. "Kim needs help. Her life has been shattered by the departure of her low-life husband. I have chosen to support her. I don't see why you can't understand this."

"I share your concern," Emily replied, "but Kim has Amy and her parents to console her. There is no need for you to play live-in therapist. Besides, we both know there is more to it than that."

"I need to do this. I'll check in with you from time to time." Sharon descended from the second floor, allowing her luggage carrier to bounce down the steps behind her. She said goodbye to Max and Maude.

Five minutes later she pulled into Kim's driveway.

Amy's welcome was less than enthusiastic. Her first response was, "You're not Daddy. When is Daddy coming home?" Her second response was, "Where is Max? Why didn't you bring Max? I want Max."

Sharon was shocked. She had not expected to be made to feel unwelcome. "Amy," she said, "I have come here to be with you and your mother for a while. I am here to help, in any way I can. I would like us to become best buddies."

Amy ran off to her room upstairs, slamming the door behind her. "I'm sorry about that," Kim said. "Amy's upset. She hasn't yet adjusted to Phil's flight. I haven't either, unfortunately. I had no idea he was having an affair. I bought all his excuses about late meetings and out-of-town conferences."

Kim fled into Sharon's arms, just before breaking down in tears. "I made the right decision to come here," Sharon said to herself.

She had second thoughts that night. Amy burst into the bedroom. "I had a bad dream," she screamed. She leaped onto the bed.

"Ouch," said Sharon.

"Aii, you are not my Daddy. Mommy, where's Daddy?"

"It's OK, Amy," Kim said. "This is Sharon. You know, Max's Mommy." Amy began to cry. She crawled over Sharon and inserted herself under the covers next to Kim.

After work the next day, Sharon returned to the Smith-Grabowski house. She left a note for Emily stating that she was taking Max for an overnight with Amy.

Max was eager for a car ride. He was in his element sniffing the air when Sharon pulled into Kim's driveway. Amy had been riding her bicycle back and forth on the sidewalk in front of the house. She abandoned it on the front lawn and ran to greet Max.

She greeted Max with a big hug. For the remainder of the day she demanded his full attention. There were frequent hugs and extended petting sessions. Max submitted to this. He recalled a conversation with his friend Ralph, a therapy dog. Ralph stressed that it is important to accept the mauling of well-intentioned strangers. Max reflected that it must be hard to be a therapy dog. He longed for a bit of personal space apart from Amy. He concluded that he had been wrong about being liked. It is possible to be liked too much.

Fortunately, Max was scheduled for drug detection patrol at the airport the next day. Sharon delivered him to Officer Oliver and returned to Kim's house.

After work, Max sought Maude's support. "Don't let Sharon take me back there," he pleaded. "Amy leaves me no peace. She's constantly hugging me. It is too much."

"Well, you could pretend you were sick. Sharon would not take you to Amy's house if you were sick."

"That's brilliant. You have such great ideas. I'll go practice." Max trotted off.

It turned out that this practice was unnecessary. Kim's parents, Tim and Vera Donnelly, called her to say that they were free for a week-long visit. Kim was not ecstatic about this. However, she could hardly say no.

The impending parental arrival made Sharon's presence untenable. Kim could not host her parents with Sharon sleeping with her in her bedroom. The Donnellys would have apoplexy. Since there were only two bedrooms in the house, her own and the bedroom usually occupied by Amy, Sharon would have to go. "Actually, this is probably for the best," Kim thought. "I appreciate Sharon's concern, but the same-sex experiment has been a bit of a dud."

Sharon took the bad news in stride. "I tried to help Kim, but it seems that I have become superfluous," she said to herself. She placed a call to Emily. "Emily, I have made a terrible mistake. I miss you so much. Is there any chance I could come back?"

* *Dealing With Cheryl.*

Sharon's Return

Sharon placed a call from Kim's house to Emily at the Smith-Grabowski residence. "Is it all right if I return for a while?" Sharon asked meekly.

"Your name is on the lease," Emily retorted acidly.

"Hardly a heartfelt invitation," Sharon thought. Upon arrival she greeted Emily with head down. Max and Maude were enthusiastic about her return. Max extended his right paw and barked softly on receiving Sharon's hand. Maude then leaped up toward Sharon, confident that Sharon would catch her. Sharon did catch her. She was grateful for the welcome accorded by her animals.

Sharon retired at once to the guest bedroom. Max and Maude continued to demonstrate to Emily how happy they were to have Sharon back. Emily retired to the master bedroom shortly thereafter.

The next morning, Emily arose an hour before Sharon so that there was no interaction between them in the kitchen. Maude noticed that Emily had relocated her toiletries to the downstairs bathroom. After the women left for work, Maude summoned Max to a conference. "Max," she said, " we need to find a way to get Sharon and Emily together again. Do you have any thoughts about how we might do this?"

"Why don't we both spread out on the guestroom bed tomorrow night? Sharon will see that there's no room for her there and will return to Emily's room," Max suggested.

"Do you really think that would work?" Maude asked. "Don't you think Sharon would just move us over on her bed and then climb in?"

"I think it's worth a try," Max responded. They put the plan into effect that evening. Maude turned out to be correct.

The next day, Emily retired to her room directly after dinner. She was carrying a paperback version of John Grisham's latest novel. Sharon watched television programs in the living room. When she turned it off, Max and Maude departed for the second floor. Upon ascent to the upstairs hallway, Sharon observed that Max and Maude had placed themselves in front of the closed door of Emily's bedroom. Max began to bark softly. Maude contributed a series of mews. Their plan was to encourage Sharon to rejoin Emily in the master bedroom.

Unfortunately, Sharon did not read the situation that way. She thought Max and Maude were asking her to open the door to Emily's room so that they could spread out on Emily's bed. Sharon hesitated to open the closed door. She was afraid Emily might not welcome an animal invasion. Instead she retreated to the guest bedroom, leaving the door open for Max and Maude, should they choose to join her.

After the departure of the women for work the next morning, Maude expressed her frustration to Max. "Nothing we have done so far has had any effect on the frigid atmosphere in our house. We need to take stronger action."

"You're right," Max replied. "My ideas have had no impact. You're the one who understands why our owners do what they do. Think hard and come up with a plan to reunite them."

Maude rose to the challenge. "Come up to the guest bedroom with me," she commanded. Max dutifully followed her up the stairs. Maude led him to the head of the bed. "Can you lift up that pillow?" she asked. Max could. He nosed it up and then away from the headboard. Sharon's pajamas were neatly folded on the spot that had been beneath the pillow. "Max, could you grab the pajamas and take them to Emily's bedroom?" Maude asked.

"Of course, no problem," Max replied.

Upon arrival in Emily's bedroom, Maude directed Max to place Sharon's pajamas beneath one of the pillows on Emily's bed. "Mission accomplished," Maude announced. "Tonight Sharon will discover that her pajamas are missing, Emily will discover that they're on her bed, and this joint discovery will jolt them into the realization that they belong together."

Initially, Maude's intuition seemed to have betrayed her. Upon discovery of Sharon's pajamas, Emily's voice reached a decibel level usually reserved for spider-detection or childbirth. "Sharon," she screamed, "what's the meaning of this?"

Sharon was planted before the TV. "What's wrong?" she shouted back.

Emily was furious. "What makes you think you can just move back into my bed? That takes some nerve."

"I don't know what you're talking about," Sharon replied.

"Come up here," Emily demanded. When Sharon entered Emily's room, Emily lifted the pillow on her bed to display the pajamas resting there.

"Emily, I swear I did not do this. I don't know how my pajamas wound up under your pillow."

Emily realized that Sharon seemed to be sincere in her denial. Was this apparent sincerity genuine? She picked up the pajamas to return them to Sharon, but she grabbed them in the wrong place. "Eeuw, dog drool," she exclaimed. "Max, are you responsible for this?"

Max and Maude had been watching from just inside the bedroom door. Max bowed his head apologetically as if he had been caught stealing sausages off the kitchen counter.

Sharon was touched by this expression of love from her animals. "You know Emily, it is touching how Max and Maude have been plotting to reunite us. It seems they are anxious to reinstate the old sense of family we formerly enjoyed."

"They are such good people," Emily said., "I really think of them as human beings in other forms. Perhaps we should take their advice."

Emily looked at Sharon. Sharon looked at Emily. They both started to speak. Sharon stopped, allowing Emily to proceed. "Sharon, I may have been too harsh on you. I should have been more supportive of your efforts to console Kim. I just couldn't accept the idea that you had left my bed for hers."

"It was a mistake," Sharon replied. "I tend to get carried away. No half measures for me. I just hope that you can forgive me ."

Max and Maude exchanged glances. Both smiled, as if to say "This is a most welcome development".

Harmony Restored

Sharon had resumed her position within the Smith-Grabowski family. All was well on Thursday night. Emily and Sharon were at opposite ends of the sofa, with Max in between and Maude on Sharon's lap. The programs on the local public television channel had been of high quality.

A spokesperson interrupted the current program to deliver a pitch for viewer support of TV 7. Emily hit the mute button on the remote. "Sharon," she said, "we should celebrate our reunion in some way. How about a weekend getaway?"

"Why not? " Sharon replied. "Oh wait, Sanderson's Sluggers have a game Saturday afternoon. The team really relies on me. League rules state that there must be at least four women on the field at all times. Moreover, the pitcher must be a woman. That means me, I'm afraid. I am the only woman on the team who can throw a softball consistently over the plate. The upside of all this is that my contributions to the Sluggers gives me some status within Sanderson Financial Services, Inc.

On Saturday the lead-off batter for Sudgkin Supplies dug in at the plate. Emily watched from the spectators' bench along the third-base line. Max sat on the ground in front of her.

The Supplies' batter dribbled a foul behind the spectator bench. "I'm on it, " Max declared, running quickly to the ball. He tried to close his jaws on the ball. It was too large. Max scowled at it. "This is not a proper ball," he concluded. "How would Maude deal with this situation?" he wondered. "Why, she would bat the ball with her paws." Max propelled the ball forward, first with his right front paw and then with his left. "Ouch," he said, "this is not a soft ball."

The third baseperson arrived on the scene. She began by petting Max on the head. She then thanked Max for his attempt at retrieval. Max barked softly to acknowledge the praise. The third baseperson picked up the ball. "Yuck," she exclaimed. The ball had acquired a coating of dog saliva. She dropped the ball on the infield dirt and rolled it around with her foot.

Sharon's team came to bat in the bottom of the first inning. Sharon entered the right-side batter's box. She dropped a bunt down the third base line. "They'll never get me," she thought as she sprinted toward first base. Her stride was a bit off, however. She was going to land just short of the bag, Sharon stretched her left leg in order to reach the bag. This was a mistake. She felt a twinge as her left foot made contact with the surface of the bag. "A cramp?" she asked herself hopefully. Alas, no. It was a hamstring injury. Sharon remained on the ground for a minute. Two male teammates escorted her off the field, ensuring that no weight was placed on her left leg.

Sharon watched the remainder of the first inning alongside Emily. "Let's go home," she said. Sharon waved to her teammates. Leaning heavily on Emily, she returned to her nearby car.

Back home, Sharon hobbled to the living-room sofa. Emily left to shop at the nearby food market. Max left through the pet flap to check on traffic in the backyard. The front doorbell rang. Sharon hopped to the door.

On the other side was a man in a khaki shirt and pants. There was a shiny badge on his shirt pocket. He carried a tool box in his left hand. "Good afternoon madam, I am Sam Brown from the State Department of Inspections," he said. "There have been a number of hot-water heater explosions in the area, I am here to examine your heater to make sure it is safe to use."

"Oh, OK," Sharon replied. She pointed to the door to the basement as she collapsed again on the sofa.

Sam banged on the heater briefly. He then returned upstairs. "Your heater is fine," he said, "there's nothing to worry about there. Could I trouble you for a glass of water?"

"Sure," Sharon replied, "there are glasses in the cabinet to the right of the sink. Forgive me for not getting up. I am nursing a pulled hamstring."

Sam entered the kitchen. He opened his tool box and placed it on the counter. It contained only one hammer and one screwdriver. There was space to add any small items of value he might discover. Sam looked at the espresso machine. It was too large to fit. Back in the corner was a butcher block containing five knives. Sam pulled one from the block. "Sabatier," he said to himself. He transferred the block containing the knives to his tool box.

Sam had not noticed the presence of the Persian on the cat bed in the corner. Maude had observed the theft. When Max entered the kitchen to head for his water dish, Maude said "Max, there has been a violation of homestead security. A man dressed in khaki stole the knives that Emily swears by. He placed them in the tool box he was carrying."

Max charged into the living room, anxious to reestablish security within the Smith-Grabowski house. Unfortunately, Sam had left two minutes earlier. The front door was closed.

Max barked at the front door, demanding that it be opened. Sharon was not pleased. "Use the pet flap in the kitchen if you have to go out, Max," she commanded. Maude then placed herself in the kitchen doorway. She commenced a series of very loud "meows." Sharon found Maude's pitch extremely annoying. She arose carefully and limped to the kitchen. Maude leaped onto the counter to occupy the space where the Sabatier knives had been. She spun around, "meowing" to indicate the absence of the knives.

Sharon found this behavior perplexing. Why was Maude putting on this display? The problem was that Emily was the resident chef and Sharon normally paid little attention to activities in the kitchen. She did not realize that the knives were missing.

Emily returned with two bags of groceries. Maude repeated her act, calling attention to the absence of the block of knives. Emily caught on at once. "Sharon, what happened to my Sabatiers?" she asked.

"Oh my God, I see it now," Sharon said in some agitation. "That 'water-heater inspector' was a thief. He had a tool box with him. He must have placed our knives in it after getting a drink of water. I'll notify the police. Why don't you let Max out the front door? He appears to have picked up Sam's scent."

Max had indeed picked up Sam's scent. He emerged from the house, following Sam's trail down the sidewalk to the right. Two houses down, Sam had just engaged the front doorbell. There was no response. He turned away to try the next house in line. Max closed quickly on him, announcing impending mayhem. Emily was not far behind.

Sam swung his tool box at Max. Max had anticipated such a move. He leaped high above the swinging box, clamping down on Sam's forearm. Sam howled in pain, dropping the tool box.

Emily arrived on the scene. She opened the tool box. It was empty. Sam was screaming about his injured arm, threatening to have Max put to death. A police car arrived. Charlie Oliver emerged and greeted Max warmly. Sam realized he was in trouble.

"There has been a misunderstanding here, Officer," Sam explained. "This dog mistook me for a burglar, trying to enter that house. I am willing to forgive his attack on me."

Max meanwhile took up a position behind Sam's car. He began his "contraband in there" barks. Oliver respected Max's testimony. He opened the front door of the car and released the trunk latch. Emily's block of knives was in the trunk, along with valuable items from several other houses. Charlie produced a biscuit for Max and handcuffs for Sam.

Kids Are Not Welcome Here

It was Saturday morning. Sharon and Emily were in the kitchen preparing to host a brunch-time meeting of the AAUW Annual Book Sale Committee. There were several items on the agenda: 1) selection of volunteers to transport and arrange donated books; 2) appointment of persons to price the volumes for sale; and 3) arrangement of browsing tables and cash-transaction booths within the Marvin A. Hurd Elementary School gymnasium. Gale Roberts had called earlier to say she would be unable to attend. Her eight-year-old had come down with a bug of some sort. Shortly thereafter Frances Paduro also cancelled. The five-woman committee was down to three.

Bernice Rahm arrived at the appointed time. However, she was accompanied by two energetic offspring. She sensed dismay and quickly apologized. "I hope you don't mind. Audrey and Billy are really good kids. I thought Paul would be at home to take care of them. Unfortunately his boss called and he had to go in to the office."

Max liked kids. Compared to adults they were uncomplicated. He watched as three-year-old Billy approached Sharon. Sharon was sitting on the end of the living room sofa with Maude snoozing on her lap. Billy grabbed Maude's tail and tried to separate it from Maude's body. Maude screamed in protest. Billy released the tail and commenced to bawl. Bernice and Sharon sought to comfort him. Maude was ignored.

Maude left Sharon's lap and leaped to the windowsill overlooking the front yard. Billy gave chase, reaching up in an attempt to recapture Maude's tail. Maude abandoned the window ledge in favor of a safe position behind the sofa. Billy attempted to follow but the sofa was too close to the wall behind.

Maude was outraged. "Why is there a national registry of sexual predators but no list of known cat-tail pullers?" she asked.

Max had no answer. However, he sensed that his buddy Maude was in distress. Max resolved to relieve that distress. He had played hide-and-seek with Sharon on many occasions. His role always had been that of "seeker" and not "hider." Max realized that he needed to change roles in order to divert Billy's attention from Maude.

Max approached Billy. He barked softly, turned and ran into the bedroom. Billy gave chase. Max hid on the far side of the bed. Billy looked around. He seemed to be puzzled. Max scratched at the floor. Billy followed the sound. He smiled on finding Max. Billy reached out toward Max. Max expected to be petted. Instead Billy grabbed his left ear and tugged. Max howled and ran back into the living room.

"What have you been up to, Max?" Emily asked. "I've been trying to direct the little monster's attention away from Maude," he wanted to say. "But it seems that no good deed goes unpunished."

"Go lie down on your bed," Emily commanded. The conversation in the living room returned to the logistics of running a book sale.

Audrey found the conversation boring. She left for the kitchen intent on "cooking" something. Max cringed, but Audrey ignored him. She approached the stove and turned two of the knobs. Max immediately smelled gas. He barked urgently. "Be quiet, Max," commanded Sharon. Max disobeyed. The fumes were becoming worse. He returned to the living room, barking furiously. Bernice became concerned. Was Max indicating that something had happened to darling Audrey? The women entered the kitchen, noticed the fumes, turned off the stove and opened the back door.

No one condemned Audrey for endangering the household. "This is not right," Max thought. He singled out Audrey and began to growl. Audrey recoiled and screamed bloody murder. Emily's sympathies were with Max. Audrey was a brat who merited a growl or two. However, she was most anxious to maintain harmony within the AAUW committee. She chastised Max for his growling. Max was exiled to the cellar.

At dinnertime Max was released from exile. He assumed the "penitent sinner" posture. "Forgive me, I have sinned, but now I am anxious to atone for my sins".

It provoked the desired response. "Max, I think we have been too hard on you. It's no walk in the park dealing with brats like Billy and Audrey. A rawhide treat is in order."

Max modestly accepted his reward. He turned to Maude, who interrupted her self-cleaning routine to thank him for distracting Billy. "Virtue is its own reward," Max thought. "But it is nice to have this virtue recognized."

Onyx

The name "Onyx" was stamped on the collar worn by the black cat that limped into the Smith-Grabowski backyard. In an earlier life, Onyx had been a well-cared-for house cat. However, she had been cast aside and forced to forage for food and drink. Onyx clearly was losing the battle for survival. She was extremely malnourished. Her fur was matted. There were claw marks on her body, mementos from larger, more vicious, competitors..

Maude responded to Onyx's cries for help. She emerged slowly from the pet flap in the kitchen door. Onyx regarded her hopefully. "You look hungry," Maude began, "follow me inside and I will get you some food." Maude turned and reentered the kitchen. Onyx remained frozen in place.

Maude alerted Max to the problem. Max thought for a moment. "Where is your food dish?" he asked Maude. "On the counter top. The dish is half full."

"Can you leap onto the counter and push the dish to the edge?"

"Of course, I can do that," Maude replied, "but what good will it do?"

"Leave the rest to me," Max said.

Max left Maude to accomplish her assigned task. He trotted into the living room. Circling around the footstool Sharon had placed in front of the sofa, he nudged it slowly into the kitchen. Once there, he pushed the footstool to a position beneath Maude's food dish. Max then hopped onto the footstool, grasped the dish between his teeth, and lowered himself to the kitchen floor.

Max readjusted his grip on the dish and headed for the pet flap. "Max wait. Stop." Maude demanded.

Max placed the dish on the floor. "My master's voice, I must obey," Max replied, with a level of sarcasm seldom achieved by a dog.

"If you go head first through the flap, it will scrape the cat food off the dish. You need to back through the opening," Maude instructed. Max executed a 180-degree turn and made a not-too-graceful entrance into the backyard.

Onyx was frightened. She had experienced life-threatening encounters with dogs before, and this one was approaching backwards. This obviously was a very sneaky dog. Onyx fled to the maple tree. She extended her front paws in preparation to climb the tree. But she was too weak. She turned to face the imminent attack.

Max placed the dish on the ground. He barked softly to deny malicious intent and retreated to the kitchen.

"Well done, Max," Maude said. She returned to the backyard. "It's safe to eat," she announced. She turned and passed back through the pet flap. Back in the kitchen Maude listened for signs of activity in the backyard. Onyx cautiously approached the food dish and then rapidly consumed its contents.

Maude again passed through the pet flap, followed by Max. Onyx sprang back when she saw Max. "I live with Max," Maude said, "He's a friend. He won't hurt you. Follow me into the kitchen and we will get you some water."

Onyx paused, seemingly deep in thought. "The unknown is scary, but the status quo is a death sentence," she concluded. Onyx pushed the pet flap aside and moved into the kitchen. Maude and Max repeated their push-and-grab routine with Maude's water bowl. Onyx felt better after hydration. She spotted Maude's bed in the corner and checked in.

Two hours later, Sharon and Emily returned from work to find a third animal in the house. Onyx awakened quickly. She fled into the living room, conducted a brief survey, and selected the area beneath the sofa as a suitable hiding place.

Maude followed Onyx. "Emily and Sharon are in charge here," she explained. "They will protect you and feed you."

Onyx hesitated. She had not encountered kindness during her days as a homeless cat. However, she appreciated Maude's concern for her welfare. Onyx emerged from her hiding place.

Sharon produced salmon-flavored treats for Onyx and Maude. Onyx began to revise her opinion of large two-legged mammals. Sharon observed that there was a telephone number on Onyx's collar. She shared this observation with Emily. "We should call, of course," Emily said.

Sharon then discovered that the number was no longer in service. The telephone company could provide no information about the whereabouts of Onyx's former owner. "We have a decision to make," Sharon said.

Onyx on Probation

The four-legged animals had retired for the night. Sharon had turned off the TV. "Emily, we need to talk about Onyx," Sharon began. "It seems to me that we have three alternatives: send Onyx to the local animal shelter, seek a friend or acquaintance who is willing to give her a home, or create space for her in the Smith-Grabowski household."

"You're right, eventually we will have to decide whether Onyx is to remain with us," Emily agreed. "But why not give her a trial period. She is still recovering from her ordeal as a homeless cat. We need to see what her normal personality is like. In particular, we need to see how she interacts with Max and Maude. Why don't we revisit this issue at the end of the month."

"That sounds good. Let's see what happens," Sharon replied.

On day one of the trial period, Maude was distraught. "I can't find Squeaky," she cried, "I left him next to my bed and now he has disappeared."

"I haven't seen her," Max replied, " Do you want me to help you look for her?"

"Squeaky is a 'him'," Maude insisted, "I've been all over the house, Max. Do you suppose Onyx is responsible for his disappearance?"

Onyx, when questioned, professed ignorance of Squeaky's whereabouts. Maude paced the kitchen floor anxiously until dinner time. Emily arrived. She picked up a large scoop, spread open the "king-size" dog food bag, and made a transfer into Max's bowl. Max barked to indicate that something was wrong. There in the dish, half-covered with food pellets, was Squeaky.

"Maude, come here, I've found Squeaky," Max said.

Maude initially was delighted to be reunited with her favorite toy. Upon reflection, however, her mood became increasingly dark. "All right, Max, how did Squeaky get into your dog food bag?" she demanded.

"I don't know. I swear I didn't put her—I mean him—there," Max replied.

"Well, if you didn't place him there, who did?" Maude asked. Maude and Max shared an unexpressed suspicion that it was Onyx.

On day two of the trial period, Maude passed by Max's bed in the kitchen. She recognized a familiar aroma. Upon examination she found "Temptations" treats pressed into the corners of the bed. "I must confront Max about this," she thought. But first things first." Maude consumed the cat treats.

Max wandered into the kitchen. "All right, Max," Maude said accusingly, "why did you put my "Temptations" treats in your bed?"

"Are you crazy, Maude? Why would I have anything to do with those awful-smelling fish-flavored tidbits?"

Maude judged Max to be sincere in his denial. "I guess that leaves Onyx," Maude concluded. "She seems intent on framing one of us so as to implicate the other. Do you think Onyx is trying to ruin our relationship?"

"It seems that that may be the case," Max replied.

On day three of the trial period, Max returned from Polk Park with an intense thirst. He burst into the kitchen, zeroed in on his water bowl, and extended his tongue to lap up its contents. He met resistance. There was a transparent cover protecting the water from his invading tongue. Max growled in frustration. He clawed a hole in the saran wrap with his paw and lapped up the water beneath.

Reflecting on this incident, and the others that preceded it, Max told Maude, "I don't think Onyx is trying to drive us apart. I think she is just a practical joker who can't help herself."

Max's suggestion that Onyx was by nature a practical joker received support on day four of the trial period. Emily's left slipper was found, after a short hunt, by the garage door.

There followed two days without incident. Then on day seven of the trial period, there was a puzzling development in the master bedroom. "Emily, have you become color-blind?" Sharon inquired.

Her voice displayed a measure of irritation. "What is your precious powder-blue bra doing on top of my skirt and blouse?"

"I have no idea," Emily replied. "Wait a minute. There are pink undergarments on my pile of clothes. Could we both have made mistakes about which underwear belongs with which skirt and blouse?"

"You know, this is just the latest in a series of incidents in which objects turn up in unexpected places. We had no such problems before Onyx moved in. I think we're harboring a dedicated mischief maker. What are we going to do about this?"

Sharon and Emily regarded each other in silence for a time. Emily then said, "Life was so predictable and harmonious before we rescued that black cat. We always knew what to expect from Max and Maude. I hate to say this, but I think we need to place Onyx in some other home."

"But Emily, look at it this way. Onyx prevents us from falling into a rut. She keeps us alert to the unexpected. This is a good thing, isn't it? Are we to evict Onyx because she is inventive and interesting? Let's sleep on the issue and see how we feel in the morning."

Probation Resolved

Maude approached Onyx at bedtime. "Onyx," she said, "I think you should suppress your instinct for playing practical jokes. Emily, in particular, appears to disapprove."

"It's just a bit of innocent fun, a pleasant diversion from the tedium of ordinary routine."

"Onyx, trust me, this is a time for harmony and the security of the ordinary course of events. Your future may depend on it," Maude said sternly.

On Friday morning, Onyx pursued Emily and Sharon as they moved through the kitchen toward the garage door. As they passed the stove, Onyx began a screeching that caused birds to take flight and chipmunks to scatter in the backyard. Sharon and Emily simultaneously lectured Onyx about the harm caused by ear-splitting screams.

Onyx responded by jumping up and down in front of the stove. "Wait a minute, Emily," Sharon said. "What's wrong, Onyx?" She looked down at Onyx's wild gyrations, and then up toward the stove. There was a substantial flame emerging from one of the front burners. "Omigod," Sharon exclaimed, "I forgot to turn off the burner after frying our eggs. Well-spotted, Onyx."

Emily removed her hand from the garage doorknob and turned back to see Sharon reward Onyx with a "Temptations" tuna treat.

"You know, Emily, that black cat is really intelligent." Sharon said. "She saw that we were about to leave with the burner still on."

* * * * *

A whiskey sour before dinner was a Friday night tradition. Emily and Sharon agreed that this was an appropriate way to mark the transition from workweek to weekend. Her glass now empty, Emily left to prepare dinner. Since the preparation involved only the microwave oven, Sharon remained attentive to TV 4's presentation of "facts" served up by our leading politicians. She winced every time she heard "the fact of the matter is . . ."

Max and Onyx were in the kitchen when Emily arrived. Max had wolfed down his dinner. He then turned to attack the contents of his water bowl. Then there occurred what sounded like a muffled bark emanating from the backyard. Emily, whose attention was on the microwave process, gave it no thought. Max, in his role as head of household security, elected to investigate. He swiveled his head away from the water bowl. A saliva-infused spray described an arc from bowl to pet flap. Max padded nonchalantly through it on his way to the backyard.

Onyx took up a position in front of the saliva-coated area of the kitchen floor. She commenced to "meow" loudly.

"What's the matter Onyx?" Emily asked, peering over one shoulder. Onyx raised her right front paw and pointed to the slippery area. Now that it was called to her attention, Emily could see that the area in question had a shine lacked by the rest of the kitchen floor. She removed this safety hazard by applying a mop and some paper towels to the area.

Max returned. He reassured the family that all was well. "The household is secure, thanks to the efforts of its leader," he said modestly. It was Onyx, however, who received praise from the persons really in charge. It was becoming clear that Onyx had a role to play in the Smith-Grabowski household. She was proving adept at identifying threats to the safety of the family.

That night, Sharon and Emily fell asleep in their bed with Maude between them. Max had been curled up between their legs at the foot of the bed. After the second involuntary kick from Emily, Max chose to sleep on the rug. He did not realize that he was in the direct path from Sharon's side of the bed to the bathroom. At 3 a.m., Sharon was forced to compensate for an earlier excess of wine. She was about to step on Max when Onyx issued a warning in the form of a shriek. "Thank you, Onyx," Sharon said, "I might have turned an ankle there."

"Not to mention damage to the innocent dog," Max grumbled.

Saturday morning featured extended sleep time for Emily and Sharon. Max, too, enjoyed a snooze at the foot of their bed. Onyx and Maude paced the kitchen floor, waiting for breakfast to be served. Onyx became tired of waiting. She emerged into the backyard, on the lookout for rodents, birds and small animals.

Helmut, an ill-tempered Rottweiler, spotted her from the sidewalk. Helmut was noted for an intense dislike of cats. He charged into the yard, pulling up short as Onyx disappeared through the pet flap.

Onyx was panting from her sprint back to the kitchen. Maude prepared to replace her in the backyard. She was intent on a session of "bird-hunting." Onyx called out a sharp warning, "Mad Dog, watch out!" Maude cautiously stuck her head through the flap. There indeed was a dog waiting for Onyx to reappear. Maude shifted quickly into reverse. Helmut barked twice in frustration, and then retreated to the sidewalk to seek other cats to terrorize.

Maude felt the beginning of a bond forming. "Onyx," she said, "you just saved one of my lives."

The four-legged residents met after breakfast. Max took the floor. "Onyx, you know that I am in charge of household security in this place. It would seem that you have assumed the position of "inspector in charge of accident prevention."

Maude interrupted at this point. "This is all well and good, but what exactly is my role in this group?"

"Why, Maude," Max replied, "It's obvious. You are 'Chancellor of the Smith-Grabowski Institute for Advanced Study.' In short, you are the brains of the outfit." Maude looked down at her front paws demurely. She was pleased to have her superior intellectual powers recognized.

Emily and Sharon noticed the harmony that had developed among the resident four-legged animals. Emily admitted to Sharon that her attitude toward Onyx had changed. "At first I was put off by the pranks she played," she admitted. "However, it has become clear that she wishes no harm on her fellow residents. On the contrary, she has been continually on guard to promote our health and safety. I have no reservations about adding her to the family."

"I agree completely," Sharon replied. "Onyx has fulfilled our initiation requirements. We should plan a ceremony in her honor."

Onyx in Demand

Emily emerged from her Saturday morning shower with a towel around her head. Sharon was enjoying the ten-minute snooze awarded by a button on the bedside clock. "Sharon," Emily said, "I'm going to the animal shelter to order a new collar attachment for Onyx with our address and phone number on it."

"Good idea," Sharon mumbled into her pillow.

Emily was struck by the pungent odor of disinfectant as she entered the Millwood Animal Shelter. Evidently there had been some anxious animals with weak bladders in the room recently.

Frances Bowen, a weekend volunteer at the shelter, greeted Emily with a cheerful, "Hi, what can I do for you?"

"I'd like to have an identification tag engraved to place on my cat's collar," Emily said.

"Right," Frances said. "Let me have the information you want placed on the tag. It will be ready tomorrow morning." Emily had printed the name "Onyx" and the Smith-Grabowski address and telephone number on a card. She handed the card to Frances.

Frances looked at the card. Her brow furrowed, an indication that she felt herself to be in an uncomfortable situation. "The name 'Onyx,'" she began, "that's an unusual one. A lady was here a week or two ago asking us to be on the lookout for her missing cat. She was very upset. She said that the cat was wearing a collar on which the name 'Onyx' was inscribed. There was no address, only a telephone number.

"Unfortunately, the lady cancelled the family home landline in favor of individual cell phones. It had not occurred to her that the number on Onyx's collar then was no longer in service. Do you suppose there is any chance that your 'Onyx' might be the same cat Mrs. Sturgeon has lost?"

"Well, I don't know," Emily said. Her voice betrayed depression. "How long has Mrs. Sturgeon's Onyx been missing?"

"About a month," Frances replied. "I have her cell phone number and address here on this note she left with us. Let me make a copy for you."

Emily smiled, accepted the Sturgeon address and phone number, and returned to relay the bad news to Sharon.

"Do we have to call this Sturgeon person?" Sharon asked. "I can't imagine the house without Onyx in it. She is a great companion for us and for Max and Maude."

The four-legged animals had been listening. "Onyx," Maude inquired, "would you really consider leaving us? You are part of our family here. And it's a good family, unorthodox perhaps, but we support one another."

"If it were up to me, I never would leave. I love you guys," Onyx replied, "but our two-legged masters decide these issues. It has something to do with 'ownership.' They don't consult us."

Onyx was right. Emily and Sharon agreed that the right action to take was to inform Mrs. Sturgeon that they had Onyx. Emily placed the call. Mrs. Sturgeon arrived within the hour. She smiled broadly when she saw Onyx. Onyx, in turn, responded with a soft "meow." The two-legged animals conferred briefly. Mrs. Sturgeon then scooped up Onyx and carried her to her car.

Emily and Sharon watched them disappear. Emily had tears in her eyes. Sharon embraced her.

Max said to Maude, "I can't believe this. She just took Onyx away."

A Cure for Boredom

Maude was bored. Emily and Sharon were at work. Max was at Polk Park with Prince and his other buddies. Onyx had gone. Maude leaped up on the kitchen counter and looked out the window. There was no activity. Sharon had neglected to refill the bird feeder. "I have nothing to do," Maude said to herself, "and it is two hours before my next scheduled nap."

There were soft sounds in the yard next door. "Trudy" Dolan was talking to her toddler Alison. The Dolan family—Gertrude, Tom and Alison—had moved in the prior week. Maude decided to investigate. She peered cautiously between shrubs that separated the two yards. Trudy was sprawled onto a lawn chair. Alison was crawling on the grass. Alison spied Maude. She gurgled, blew a bubble, and headed for Maude.

Alison squeaked with delight as she patted Maude's back with her tiny hands.

"Well, that's not too bad," Maude thought. But then Alison poked her in the eye with a tiny finger. "Is this creature hostile or just clumsy?" Maude asked herself.

Alison discovered Maude's tail. After two painful yanks, Maude fled to Trudy. Maude recalled Sharon and Emily discussing the name "Gertrude."

"Did you know," Emily began, "if a child turns out to be a swan, she receives the nickname 'Trudy,' but if she turns out to be a duckling, she receives the nickname 'Gerti'?" Maude decided to apply this bit of folk wisdom. She concluded that Mrs. Dolan was a borderline Trudy at best. The mousy hair, bushy eyebrows and overbite were not very swan-like. And she could lose 20 pounds and still be overweight.

None of this mattered to Maude. Trudy encouraged her to enjoy some lap time. Maude was the recipient of a pleasant stroking session. It was interrupted by the sound of a ringing cell phone in the kitchen. Trudy had been charging it, otherwise she would have had it on her person.

Trudy left for the kitchen, unceremoniously casting Maude to the turf. Maude quickly recognized what she must do. She needed to keep Alison amused and out of trouble while her owner was occupied.

Maude noticed a tennis-ball sized rubber ball on the grass. She swatted it toward Alison. Alison giggled, scooped up the ball, tried to surround it with her mouth, realized that it did not fit, released it, and struck it sharply with her right hand. Maude intercepted it and produced a return strike. Alison was dimly aware that this was some sort of game. After slobbering over the ball for a time, she knocked it forward.

Trudy had observed the latter stages of the game from the kitchen window as she gave husband Tom instructions about ingredients to be purchased for dinner. "That is one perceptive cat," she thought. "It's as if she knew I might be leaving Alison unsupervised, and provided a distraction to keep her out of trouble. I see that the name on her tag is 'Maude'".

But then trouble arrived in the form of Ajax, a mean-tempered bulldog. Ajax advanced into the yard, spotted Maude and Alison, and barked loudly. "I wish Max were here," Maude thought. "I'll try a bluff and hope for the best." She rose up on her hind legs and produced a high-pitched hissing sound that Ajax found irritating.

He hesitated for a moment and then realized, "Hey, this is a cat. I chase cats." Ajax charged forward.

Maude feinted left and then moved quickly to the right. Ajax was a more straight-line type of runner. He applied the brakes, and was about to redirect his path toward Maude, when Trudy charged down the steps from the kitchen screaming obscenities. Ajax wanted no part of this two-legged demon. He made a quick exit to the sidewalk beyond the yard.

"Maude, you're a heroine," Trudy said. "Come inside, I have some albacore tuna I think you might like." Maude recognized the word "tuna." Her face expressed intense interest in such a snack. Trudy carried Alison into the kitchen, holding open the screen door for Maude.

Maude displayed excellent manners as she daintily consumed the tuna. Plate empty, she licked her whiskers and offered a "meow" of appreciation. She continued to look up at Trudy. "What's wrong?" she asked. "Oh, of course, let me get you some water. Maude mewed thanks as she bent over the water dish. Trudy picked up the dish that had contained the tuna. She applied a dish cloth to its surface.

Meanwhile, Alison had nudged open the door to the basement. Trudy had neglected to engage the latch that closed it. Alison was about to descend head-first down the steps. Maude conjured up an image of Onyx, the Goddess of Accident Prevention. "What would Onyx do?" she asked. Maude "meowed" loudly, gaining Alison's attention as she walked slowly behind her. Alison turned away from the inviting steps. She caught sight of Maude's twitching tail, now within reach. Alison latched onto Maude's tail. Maude suppressed a scream as she towed Alison to safety away from the open basement door.

Trudy placed the dish in the drying rack. She turned to see Maude, in obvious pain, drag Alison away from danger. "Maude," she said, "you are one insightful cat. You have a future as a well-paid toddler-minder."

Maude smiled and headed for the kitchen door. Trudy opened it. "Thank you so much. Come again any time." Maude passed through the shrubs on the way home to a long-deferred nap. She anticipated pleasant dreams during which she accepted praise for a variety of heroic exploits.

Bastet Rules

Bastet lay on a window ledge surveying the front lawn. She observed a car pull into the driveway. "This is normal," she thought, "there is no cause for concern."

Bastet's mistress emerged carrying what appeared to be a cat. "A cat!" Bastet exclaimed. "What is going on here? I don't like this one bit. There already is a cat in charge here. It is me, Bastet, daughter of Isis. I am the slayer of the sacred snake. Two-legged animals participate in festivals in my honor. I will eliminate any creature that challenges my authority." Bastet leaped down from the ledge, arched her back, and practiced her menacing hiss.

Sarah Sturgeon introduced Onyx to Bastet. Bastet hissed in response. She turned away, entered the kitchen, and took up a position in front of her food dish. Her posture indicated that any animal that approached would be treated as a scratching post. Sarah noticed the display of antagonism. She lectured Bastet on the virtues of tolerance, amiability, and hospitality. Bastet hissed at her.

Onyx was frightened. This no longer was the home environment she had known. "This replacement cat the Sturgeons have acquired is not disposed to share food, water or territory," she thought. "She enjoys chasing me whenever she sees me. She is huge, with sharp claws. I try to keep out of her way, but I've been scratched on more than one occasion."

"There are only two situations in which I feel relatively safe. If Sarah or Alan is present, Bastet will not attack me. She is smart enough to know that if the Sturgeons are forced to choose which cat to keep, she might be the loser. My other secure place is on top of the refrigerator. There's just enough room there for a small cat like me. Bastet would not fit between the top of the refrigerator and its enclosure. This is not the most pleasant of places for naps, but safety is more important than comfort." Onyx did not enjoy those times when Sarah and Alan both were away and she was trapped above the refrigerator.

"I miss Maude," Onyx said to herself. "Not every cat is a dictator-wannabee." Onyx's thoughts turned to Max. "If Max were here, he would teach that bully a lesson." Onyx entered into a daydream in which Max clamped his jaws on the fur on the back of Bastet's neck, shook her violently, and tossed her out the open kitchen door.

Onyx's reverie was interrupted by the arrival of Sarah. Bastet had been watching Onyx, hoping she would descend. When she became aware of Sarah's presence, she assumed an air of innocence. Sarah was not fooled. She realized that Bastet had forced Onyx to seek security on top of the refrigerator. "Bastet," she announced, "it's time for some outdoor activity." She picked up the descendant of Isis and deposited her in the backyard.

Sarah then returned to Onyx. She lifted her down from her hiding place. Onyx was trembling. "This will not do," Sarah declared.

That evening, the Bastet-Onyx relation was the sole topic of discussion at the Sturgeon dinner table. "The two cats just don't get along," Sarah said. "Bastet was fine before Onyx returned. She was the unchallenged protector-goddess of the house. In her mind, she was responsible for the absence of rodents, snakes and birds on the property. She even had begun to branch out into lap-sitting activities. But when Onyx returned, Bastet's worst characteristics emerged. She has become a sadistic bully. It's not fair to Onyx to place her in a situation of constant terror. I think we should decide which of the two cats to keep.

"But have we given them enough time to adjust to one another?" Alan asked. "Perhaps it just takes a bit of time for them to get used to sharing the house."

"From what I've seen," Sarah replied, "Bastet shows no evidence of developing any tolerance for Onyx."

"OK, then, which cat has to go?" Alan asked.

"I'm sure the women who rescued Onyx would love to have her back," Sarah said. "There were tears in their eyes when I took her away. Shall I call them to see if they would take her back?"

The Perfect Dog

It was Saturday morning. Max was on drug patrol at the airport. Sharon and Emily were shopping to update their wardrobes. Maude and Onyx were chatting about life at the Smith-Grabowski residence, and about Max in particular.

"You know, Maude," Onyx observed, "Max is quite reasonable . . . for a dog. Yesterday he had an itch that he could not reach by biting or scratching. I made a fuss so that Emily would see him trying to relieve the itch. Emily scratched his back for him. Max was most appreciative. He thanked me for calling the problem to Emily's attention."

"But then Emily found some anti-flea dog shampoo in a kitchen cabinet. She invited Max to participate in a bath experience. As you know, Max hates baths. It's strange, really. He loves to jump into lakes to retrieve sticks. Isn't a filled bathtub rather like a lake? At any rate, Max glared at me as Emily led him upstairs."

"I explained to him later how the special soap Emily used would eliminate itches by keeping away fleas. He thanked me again for my concern and apologized for glaring at me for my role in creating the bath experience. Max is ready to learn and willing to accept sound explanations. These are characteristics that might be manipulated to create the Perfect Dog."

"I'm thinking that The Perfect Dog, if we were to create him, would be free of fleas. Max already is on the way to becoming a Perfect Dog. With additional effort and training we might be able to elevate Max to this status."

"I don't know," Maude replied, "in my experience, attempts at social engineering often have undesirable unexpected consequences. Let me give you an example. Sharon noted that Emily had a bad habit. She kept writing checks without keeping a record in her checkbook. There occurred frequent overdrafts. Sharon engineered a change of behavior. Emily was encouraged to alter her check-writing routine. Henceforth she did not tear out a check from her checkbook until she had brought her bank balance up to date.

"This might seem to be a successful case of social engineering. But picture yourself in a grocery store check-out line behind Emily. She writes a check, but before giving it to the clerk, subtracts the amount from her prior balance to make sure the number is greater than zero.

"Emily is not quick at subtraction. She has irritated a number of grocery store patrons. Last week she was the target of insults. Emily replied in kind. Both participants received a lecture from the store manager and were placed on probation. Do you see what I mean by 'unintended consequences'?"

"I take your point, Maude," Onyx replied. "But we just need to proceed in a thoughtful way. The good that may be achieved far outweighs the mere possibility of an unintended consequence. Come on, be an optimist."

"All right, let's get back to the 'Perfect Dog' project. What changes in Max's behavior did you have in mind?"

"Well, to begin with," Onyx replied, "I think we should acknowledge that Max already possesses some excellent virtues. He protects the family and its possessions. You and I are secure from attack when Max is present. Moreover, Max contributes to the general welfare through his work as drug czar."

"Excuse me. You don't mean 'drug czar.' Max is a valued asset in anti-drug enforcement operations."

"Quite right. I misspoke. At any rate, it is clear that Max is loyal, courageous and dedicated to the elimination of evil in society. We have here the makings of the Perfect Dog. However, I submit that there still is room for improvement.

"Here comes Max now. Watch me launch the campaign for the Perfect Dog," Onyx said confidently. "Max, how was your day at the airport?"

"Very boring. There were no suspicious pieces of luggage today."

"Well, I'm sure that was because travelers are aware that you are on duty," Onyx said.

Max smiled. He glanced at Maude to make sure she agreed.

Onyx pressed on. "Max, I always have admired your hole-digging expertise. You can create a hole suitable for burying a T-bone in two minutes. It is really extraordinary." Max was pleased, but then puzzled. "What is Onyx up to?" he wondered.

"Max," Onyx inquired, "you know how Maude and I dispose of our waste products?"

"Yes," Max replied. "You cats are very fastidious. In fact, you are downright secretive. It is as if you are embarrassed by the need to perform this essential life function."

"Yes, well," Onyx continued, "it occurs to me that by altering your usual procedure you might make a great impression on Emily and Sharon." Onyx paused for effect and then pushed ahead. "Max, why not dig a hole, make a deposit, and then kick dirt back over it? You could set a new standard for your species. Imagine, dogs all over the country asking 'have you heard how Max Smith-Grabowski does his duty?'"

Max could not believe Onyx was serious. "Onyx," he said with much exasperation in his voice, "this is absurd. I cannot be expected to hold it in while I dig a hole."

"Oh, come on," Onyx replied, "all it takes is a bit of advance planning."

Maude interrupted at this point. "Onyx, I think we need to accept that whereas cats are thoughtful and plan ahead, dogs are more, um, spontaneous. Cats are cats and dogs are dogs."

"But what happened to the project to create the Perfect Dog?"

Max growled upon hearing there was such a project. There was exasperation in that growl. Was there also a bit of menace?

Onyx and Maude decided independently to check on possible rodent activity in the basement.

Paralysis of the Senses

William ("Will") Zaremba stood before carousel #1 at Millwood airport. It was not moving. Luggage was moving on carousel #2, however. Will watched the progression of bags on carousel #2 as he pretended to be waiting for action on carousel #1.

Will had a good reason for this deception. There was a suitcase designated for carousel #2 in which Will had an interest. It was a rather inconsequential looking black nylon case with a fictitious nametag attached. The case looked to be ordinary enough. But inside the nylon shell there was a second case. The inner case was filled with clothes ready for a washing machine. Between the inner case and the outer case were numerous plastic bags containing cocaine.

Will was apprehensive. There was a sniffer dog, with his handler, positioned at the head of the line at carousel #2. Will's suitcase came down the chute. The dog was unresponsive. So far so good. Will waited for his bag to pass by the dog for a second time. Again there was no response. Will advanced to carousel #2 and removed his bag.

He was wheeling the suitcase toward the baggage-claim exit when a uniformed officer approached. Officer Francis Callahan was accompanied by a Rottweiler named Manfred. Manfred commenced to bark at Will, or rather at his suitcase. Officer Callahan demanded that Will stop. Manfred continued to bark, demanding that the suitcase be examined.

Callahan pulled the inner case away from the outer case. He retrieved several plastic bags containing a white powder. A taste test confirmed that the substance was cocaine. Callahan offered Manfred a liver treat as additional police arrived to take Will into custody.

Max's shift was over. He and Officer Charlie Oliver passed by Callahan and Manfred on their way out of the airport. Manfred greeted Max cordially. There was no rivalry between them.

Max was puzzled by Manfred's discovery. "How could I have missed that?" he asked himself. Max pulled on his leash, indicating a desire to investigate the contents of the opened suitcase. Charlie obliged. Max began to sniff audibly. "Nothing." he concluded. "What is wrong with me?"

Charlie noticed Max's forlorn appearance. "It's all right, Max," Charlie said. "Everyone has an off day, once in a while. I think you should take a week or two off. I'm sure that with a bit of rest you will be back to normal as our premier drug detector."

A depressed Max padded into the Smith-Grabowski kitchen. He nodded to Maude and collapsed on his bed.

"What's wrong, Max?" Maude asked.

"I messed up. I missed a bag containing drugs. Manfred saved the day. He called attention to the drug dealer before he could leave the building."

"That's OK, Max." Maude said, "nobody bats 1000. That probably was the only bag that got past you."

Emily arrived to distribute dog food and cat food. Max rose, stuck his nose above the Kibbles 'n Bits and sighed heavily. He could not smell his dinner. "Oh well," he thought, "I will gulp it down anyway." This only deepened Max's state of depression. He found that he could not taste his dinner either.

After dinner, all three animals retired to the backyard for some fresh air. Onyx and Maude challenged Max to identify the most recent visitor to the maple tree near the sidewalk. Max was disconsolate. "I can't tell," he complained, "All I have left are my senses of sight and hearing. The world has lost its olfactory complexity."

Onyx and Maude conferred. "We rely on Max to protect us," Onyx said. "It doesn't much matter that his senses of smell and taste are impaired. What counts is his ability to see and hear. I think we should arrange tests of these senses just to reassure ourselves."

"Good idea," Maude replied. "Go upstairs and thump on a closed door. Let's see if Max hears you."

Onyx did as Maude suggested. Max responded at once. "What was that noise from upstairs?" he demanded. Max quickly ascended the stairs. Onyx praised him for his keen sense of hearing. Max was pleased.

"Let's go outside," Maude urged. The three animals congregated on the patio in the backyard. "You stay here," Maude directed Max. "I will go to the sidewalk and raise one front paw. You tell me which paw it is." Maude scampered into position. "OK, Max, which paw have I raised?" she asked.

"Your paws are all on the ground. What kind of game is this?" he asked.

"Very good, Max. There is nothing wrong with your vision," Maude concluded.

"We are reassured by the results of these tests, Max," Onyx said. I am sorry you have lost your sense of smell. I hope it returns soon. The important thing is that you are able to continue your excellent service as Chief of Household Security."

That evening, Charlie Oliver placed a call to Sharon. "I'm concerned about Max," he said. "He is still a young dog. And yet he's lost his sense of smell. Does he appear to lack energy?"

"Max seems to be depressed rather than tired," Sharon said. "I believe he blames himself for failure in his role as drug-detector. Let's hope the loss of smell is temporary."

"Hopefully, it is," Charlie replied. "We have arranged for Max to take a two-week leave of absence. But as a precaution, I think it would be wise to take him to a vet."

Sharon did so the next day. Vet Veronica Bailey considered the options. "I have encountered a couple of cases where exposure to bleach produced a temporary loss of the sense of smell," she said. "Has Max been exposed to bleach recently?"

Sharon replied that Max never had shown interest in laundry operations. In the absence of knowledge of a cause, Veronica prescribed a course of antibiotics for Max, just in case he had acquired a bacterial infection.

There followed a period of waiting. Maude and Onyx surrounded Max as each meal was delivered. For several days, each time Max looked up from his bowl he shook his head from side from side. Then on a Saturday morning when he normally would be on drug-detection duty, Max discovered that he could trace the history of recent visits to the yard's maple tree.

The spring returned to Max's walk. He engaged Emily and Sharon in paw-shaking activity. Encouraged by Max's new vitality, Emily arranged a test. She led Max to the kitchen and demanded that he stay there. She then placed a liver treat beneath a pillow on the living-room sofa. Emily sat on the sofa. She called Max for an ear-scratching session.

Max allowed a preliminary scratch, and then stuck his nose under the pillow. He repressed his instinct to swallow the liver treat immediately. "I should chew this awhile to see if I can taste it," he said to himself. "Aha," he concluded.

Max smiled at Emily and hopped up onto the sofa beside her. "Max, you know that is not allowed," Emily said. She was about to order him to vacate his position next to her on the sofa. But this seemed to be such a special occasion. "Max, we all are delighted that you have come to your senses," she said happily.

A Visit from Ollie

Sharon was the first home from work. "Aha," she thought, "I get to choose the pre-dinner drink tonight." She brought down the vodka and white vermouth. Task completed, she greeted Emily as the door from the garage opened. Emily was carrying a large object. Closer inspection revealed that it was a cage. There was a blue-colored bird perched on a rod inside. Emily placed the cage on the kitchen table.

"Ollie wanna cracka," the bird announced.

"Oh, that's cute, Emily, does he say anything else?" Sharon asked sarcastically.

"Ima pretty bird," Ollie responded.

"Emily, what's going on?" Sharon demanded. "You know Maude and Onyx will be outraged. There is no way that they would tolerate the presence of a budgie in the house."

"But perhaps we can convince them it is a parakeet," Emily suggested.

"Not funny," Sharon replied, "'budgie', 'parakeet,' what's the difference?"

"Don't get excited," Emily said. "I agreed to pick up Ollie at the pet store and keep him overnight. Tomorrow he will be a farewell present for Julie Thompson, who is moving away after ten years at the firm. If things go as I hope, I will be appointed to replace her as 'paralegal associate.' I then will receive a small percentage of the profits distributed at the annual partners' meeting."

Sharon grunted grudging approval. She poured out vodka martinis. She and Emily prepared to adjourn to the living room for some well-earned relaxation. Their progress was interrupted by the arrivals of Onyx, Maude and Max through the pet flap.

Ollie the budgie commenced to flap his wings and squawk. As Sharon had predicted, Onyx was outraged by the presence of a bird in the kitchen. Actually the outrage was directed more at the cage than at

Ollie himself. "If only there were no cage," Onyx thought. She licked her lips at the prospect.

"Why are you so upset, Onyx?" Max asked.

"It's a bird. It is in our nature to chase them. Why is it that to pursue mice is 'good,' but to pursue birds is 'bad'?"

"Beats me," Max replied. "I myself have no inclination to chase either mice or birds. '*Laissez faire*,' as the French say."

Emily was not pleased by Onyx's display. "Knock it off, Onyx." She continued into the living room, hinting that there might be treats available there. Max led the animals to their usual begging positions in front of the sofa.

Emily and Sharon sipped their drinks as Max gulped down a liver treat. His look indicated disappointment that it was such a small treat. Emily delivered a second.

The martinis produced the desired reduction of stress. Neither Emily nor Sharon noticed the departure of the animals.

Suddenly there was much squawking from Ollie in the kitchen. It was followed by a loud thumping sound. Emily left the living room to investigate. The bird cage was on the kitchen floor. Ollie was unhurt. Nevertheless, he expressed freely his terror at being attacked.

"Omigod, Ollie, what has happened here?" Emily asked. She replaced the cage on the table.

"Some creature must have pushed the cage over the edge," Sharon observed. "That would take considerable force. Max, where are you?"

Max was in the corner on his bed. Onyx and Maude had fled through the pet flap. Max saw no reason to join them.

"Max, how did the bird cage get onto the floor?" Emily demanded. Max shrugged to indicate that he had no idea how such an accident could have happened. He rubbed his body against Emily's legs. "OK, Max, I believe you," Emily said. She then hid behind the partially open garage door to await developments.

Onyx reentered the kitchen through the pet flap. She observed that the irritating bird was back on the table, and the kitchen otherwise was empty. Sharon was on her second martini in the living room. Emily was nowhere in sight. Onyx leaped onto the table, emitted her most intimidating "meow," and struck the cage with her left front paw.

This was a mistake. Emily had been listening. She emerged from behind the garage door. "Onyx, get down from there," she shouted.

Onyx leaped down from the table, bounced once, and was through the pet flap before Emily could catch her. Emily turned to reassure Ollie. "Ollie wanna cracka," he said. Emily produced a cracker for him, checked his water supply, and carried the cage upstairs into the master bedroom. She placed a towel over the cage. "Night-night, Ollie," she crooned, closing the bedroom door behind her.

Onyx and Maude were not pleased at that evening's sleeping arrangements. They were accustomed to sleeping on the unoccupied areas of the king-sized bed in the master bedroom. Tonight they were excluded in favor of a "talking" bird.

"This is wrong," said Onyx. "Let's scratch on the bedroom door until they let us in." Maude wasn't sure this was a good idea. Onyx began a door-scratching operation on her own. She was not dissuaded by shouts of "Go away," from behind the closed door.

Eventually the door opened to reveal a furious Sharon. "Onyx, look at these scratch marks," she shouted. She bent down to pick up Onyx. Onyx quickly darted down the stairs and hid under the living room sofa.

Sharon turned to Maude, scooped her up, and deposited her on the basement stairs. She closed the door, leaving Maude in the basement to contemplate her role in the plot against Ollie.

Emily also was furious at this point. She stormed downstairs, demanding that Onyx come out of hiding. Onyx chose to remain undetected under the sofa. Annoyed, Emily joined Sharon in the kitchen for an impromptu tea party.

Emily had failed to close the bedroom door as she left for the first floor. Onyx stealthily emerged from beneath the sofa. She padded upstairs and entered the bedroom. Ollie was sleeping in his cage on top of a bureau. Onyx leaped up onto the bureau. She pulled off the towel and struck the cage with her paw. Ollie responded with excited squawking. He was terrified of this black animal with luminous green eyes.

Sharon reentered the bedroom with Emily close behind her. This time Emily had the presence of mind to close the bedroom door, trapping Onyx inside.

Realizing that Sharon was angry, Onyx adopted her penitent posture, looking up at Sharon with eyes that pleaded for forgiveness. Sharon rejected the penitent-sinner schtick. "Onyx, you need to realize that Emily and I are in charge here. When we say 'cease and desist' we expect to be obeyed. You are banished to the basement for the rest of the night. No door-scratching will be tolerated. You will wait there patiently until we allow you back upstairs."

To show that she meant business, Sharon relocated the litter box to the basement.

The Baron Banished

Onyx knew that Maude regarded any intentional interruption of her morning nap to be a felony. However, this news was so important that Maude had to be informed at once. Onyx anticipated that considerable cursing would accompany the transition from restorative snooze to awareness of an irritating presence nearby. She wasn't wrong.

Maude's outburst over, Onyx announced that she had great news. "Our beloved bully, The Baron, * has been placed in confinement at the Millwood Animal Shelter. The Baron made the mistake of clawing the young son of Philip Fletcher, the owner of Fletcher's Fish Market. Fletcher had The Baron committed. The area behind the market now is free of The Baron's sadistic dictatorship. We could go to Fletcher's now," Onyx suggested. "There is nothing like a bit of halibut to perk up one's diet."

Max overheard this conversation. "Maude, I know you still have nightmares about The Baron. I should go with you just in case he's been released."

"I appreciate that, Max. Let's all go," Maude replied.

The cat population behind Fletcher's had exploded following The Baron's departure. Formerly, only The Baron himself and a couple of obedient enforcers were permitted in the area. Today twelve cats were on the scene. Half were from homes in the neighborhood, half were homeless.

Maude called Onyx for a conference. "Onyx," Maude began, "we can't let tyranny be replaced by anarchy. We need to impose democratic order on the fish-distribution process. I propose that we identify the democratically-inclined cats present. We then could consider plans for the equitable distribution of Fletcher's excess seafood."

Onyx was not convinced. "I dunno," she said, "cats just don't band together to pursue a common goal. What I recommend is benevolent rule by a thoughtful and compassionate leader. You would be perfect in that role."

If cats could blush, Maude would have done so at this point. "Onyx is very perceptive," she thought. "I am a natural leader. Moreover, my judgments are nearly always correct. I will accept this challenge."

Maude's leadership was about to be put to the test. Zeke Smith emerged from the back door of the market. Zeke was noted for his broad smile as he sliced fish fillets to order for Fletcher's customers. Currently he was carrying a pail of fish parts to the garbage cart behind the store.

Max barked as Zeke approached the cart. Zeke turned to face him. "Why would a dog be interested in the disposal of fish?" he wondered. Max barked again, more insistently this time.

Zeke put down the pail in order to pry open the lid of the garbage cart. Max placed himself between Zeke and the pail. He smiled at Zeke, offering his paw. Zeke decided it would be wise to reciprocate.

Max turned away. He applied his nose to the top of the pail. Ignoring the unpleasant odor, he lunged forward. Fish parts spilled from the overturned pail.

Zeke retreated into the store for a broom and a shovel. Maude seized the moment. She called for Max to join her. Max amiably sat down beside her. Maude placed her right foreleg across Max's shoulders. She used her left front paw to gesture toward the assembled fish-lovers.

"Fellow cats," Maude began, "form a line. When I raise my paw the first-in-line is to approach. I will give you a fish-part from the pail. Take it to the grass area in front of the fence and enjoy it. Then I will signal with my paw for the next-in-line to advance." Maude paused, pleased with her creative exercise of leadership.

The pleasure quickly passed. No line formed. Instead the cats charged the overturned pail from all directions. They completely ignored Maude, despite the fact that she was leaning on Max.

"This is depressing," Maude said. "You and I cooperate on numerous projects. Are these creatures at Fletcher's members of another species?"

"Maude," Onyx replied, "you did your best. It seems that cooperation among cats does not extend beyond a given household."

* *Fish A La Cart.*

Max Fingers a Drug Mule

Mario Bianchi spread his considerable girth over two chairs along the inner wall facing the baggage claim area. His bag had been approved for retrieval by the sniffer dog on duty. Mario lurched to his feet. He waddled to that section of the baggage carousel furthest from the dog. As Mario stooped to collect his bag, the sniffer dog became agitated.

Max was the sniffer dog on duty. His sense of smell had returned.* Max had been given a drug-detection re-test at the airport. He compiled a 100% score on the test.

Max growled and pulled on his leash, leading Officer Charlie Oliver around to the other side of the carousel. He barked twice at Mario.

"But you already examined that suitcase," Charlie admonished. Max continued to indicate that Mario was a smuggler. "All right, Max," we will open the bag for inspection." Max showed no interest in the open suitcase. He continued to growl and to bark at Mario himself.

Airport Security recently had installed a CT scanning device to thwart drug mules. Mario was unaware of this. Charlie led him into the room containing the scanner. Mario protested that he needed immediately to respond to a call of nature. Charlie was not sympathetic. Mario was introduced to the CT scanner. The result was a picture of suspicious packets in his intestinal tract. Mario was placed in a holding cell with a bucket for companionship.

"Rats," he said, regarding the bucket, "I'm damned if I do and I'm damned if I don't."

"Outstanding work, Max," Charlie said. Max beamed. This was his first identification of a drug mule.

Recognition was in order. That evening, Charlie arrived at the Smith-Grabowski residence with a citation and a tin of pâté for Max. Emily had just finished the hoagie she had purchased on the way home from the office. She was alone. Sharon was at an after-work drinks party with coworkers.

"Max, I am so proud of you. Millwood is a safer place because of your contributions to law enforcement," Emily said. Max looked down at his toes modestly, and then up to the kitchen counter where pâté was being spread on a cracker. Emily suggested that it would be appropriate for Charlie to present the snack. Max wolfed it down, responding with a growl of pleasure.

Maude and Onyx complained. "If this is a celebration, shouldn't we be included?" Onyx asked.

"Of course, I'm sure Max would want that," Emily responded, handing out two salmon-flavored treats apiece.

Emily made two cups of coffee. She led Charlie to the living room sofa. Max, Maude and Onyx surrounded them. Charlie took a sip of coffee. "This is a great dog you have here," he said, while scratching Max behind the ear. "I'll bet he's very protective of you.."

Emily smiled, recalling some of Max's exploits in the service of household security.

"So tell me, Emily, what do you like to do for fun?" Charlie asked, training his dark brown eyes upon hers.

"Well . . . ," Emily said.

Charlie pressed on. "Do you like to dance?"

"Dance . . . , " Emily began.

Charlie leaped in to fill the void. "I was thinking about the PBA affair next Saturday night," he said. "I'm sorry, PBA?" Emily queried, stalling for time.

"Oh, it's a benefit dance for the Policeman's Benevolent Association," Charlie explained.

"Omigod, he's hitting on Emily," Maude observed.

"Max," she said, "you need to set Charlie straight. He is barking up the wrong tree here."

"Barking? What tree?" asked a confused Max.

"Charlie's approaching Emily just as you approached that standard poodle in the park yesterday, Max," Maude said. "You do see how that is inappropriate, don't you? You need to save Charlie from embarrassment. Tell him that Emily is off-limits."

"How am I supposed to do that?" Max asked.

Onyx had been trying to follow this conservation. "I have an idea," she said. "There is a photo of her brother Steve upstairs. Bring it down and show it to Charlie. He will conclude that this is her boyfriend and that he should back off."

"That won't work, Onyx," Maude replied. "The police are well acquainted with our friend Steve. They know who he is. If you show Charlie the photo, he will just ask Emily how her brother is doing."

"OK, how about this?" Maude suggested. "We retrieve one of Emily's padded bras from the laundry basket and drop it on the floor in front of Charlie. Men hate them. I have heard those who wear them accused of false advertising. I don't get it, but everyone hates advertising, and false advertising (if this phrase is not redundant) is the worst."

"I'm on it," Max declared. He nosed through the laundry basket, located a bra, and carried it to the living room. On Maude's signal, Max waved the bra in front of Charlie.

Emily grabbed it. Her cheeks flushed. "Max, what is the meaning of this?" She didn't wait for an answer. She took direct action, escorting Max to the basement. Maude and Onyx remained in the living room, feigning innocence.

"Well that clearly didn't work," Onyx observed. Charlie had placed his right arm along the top of the sofa, ready to surround Emily if given any encouragement.

"What do we do now, Onyx?' Maude asked. Onyx had nothing to contribute. Fortunately, the silence was broken by Sharon, who made a noisy, semi-inebriated entrance into the kitchen. Emily arose from the sofa to check on her. Sharon embraced her warmly. This action was not lost on Charlie.

"What am I doing here?" he asked himself. "Ten minutes more and I might have been subject to a sexual harassment lawsuit."

On the way to the front door, he called out to the still-entwined couple. "Thanks for the coffee, Emily. Tell Max I will pick him up for drug-detection duty next Saturday."

* *Paralysis of the Senses.*

Sharon Makes Some Bad Choices

Emily and Sharon had just left for work. At the time of their departure, the atmosphere in the Smith-Grabowski house was decidedly cool. "There is trouble in paradise," Maude announced to Max and Onyx.

"Did you sense that too?" Onyx asked. "I think Emily and Sharon have had a fight."

"You two are imagining things," Max interjected. "The usual morning routine was followed. Most importantly, we were fed well and on time."

"I was the only one of us in the master bedroom last night," Maude said. "I overheard a most disturbing conversation this morning. Emily was very upset. She accused Sharon of being cold and aloof. 'Sharon,' she said, 'there is no warmth here, no reciprocity... I feel like an attendant at a petrol station who is called upon to apply jumper cables to a dead battery.'"

"'Petrol station?'" Sharon retorted. "'Here in Millwood we have gas stations. You've been watching too many PBS British sitcoms.'"

"'OK, forget it. You clearly would prefer to wallow in self-pity. I tried to be here for you, but clearly my concern doesn't matter.'"

"This is the point at which Sharon apologizes," Maude thought. Maude was wrong. Sharon stormed into the bathroom, slamming the door. Maude approached Emily, arching her back to be stroked. Emily was preoccupied. She threw on a robe and descended to the kitchen to prepare breakfast.

Max put on his "thank you" face as Emily filled his bowl. She then turned to the refrigerator, removed the carton of eggs, and began the scrambling process. "Eggs, Sharon?" she asked, when Sharon entered the kitchen.

"No eggs," Sharon replied, traversing the kitchen to the garage. She ignored the concerned animals. The sound of a garage door opening was followed by the roar of an engine. Sharon was on the way to her job at Sanderson Investments.

Sharon didn't return to the Smith-Grabowski house at the normal hour. Emily had made martinis in the hope of a reconciliation. It was nine o'clock when Sharon staggered into the kitchen, fortunate not to have encountered a police cruiser on her way home from Peter's Pub.

"Sharon, this isn't like you," Emily said, taking Sharon by the arm to her preferred corner of the living room sofa. "I've been fired," Sharon sobbed.

Emily initially was unable to respond. Eventually she said "But I thought you were doing so well at Sanderson Investments."

"I was for a while, but I made some bad choices recently," Sharon replied. "The big shots at Sanderson recommend that we steer investors to mutual funds created by the firm itself. I thought I could do better by selecting individual companies for my clients. I was wrong. One of my picks was hit with an antitrust suit, another lost a factory to a suspicious explosion, and a third lost expected contracts to a competitor in South Korea. I would have done better recommending the purchase of 'Spiders.'"

"'Spiders'?" Max asked Maude. "I didn't know those arachnids had value."

"C'mon, Max, they eat mosquitoes and flies. Surely that is something of value," Maude replied.

Sharon noted that Emily seemed puzzled. She explained that "Spiders represent shares of the Standard and Poors' collection of 500 stocks." Unfortunately I did not place my clients either in Spiders or in mutual funds." Sharon's half-smile was replaced by a frown. She collapsed against Emily and commenced to sob.

Maude leaped onto her lap. Onyx rubbed against her legs, and Max placed his jaw on her thigh. The sobbing continued despite their best efforts.

The next day Emily informed the law firm of Klinghofer, Cohen, Esposito and Smart that she had a sore throat and would be working at home on two estate-tax forms. She made herself available when Sharon finally dragged herself downstairs. Over breakfast she asked Sharon if there was anything that she could do. Maude and Onyx "meowed" to indicate their desire to help. Max contributed to the supportive atmosphere by slobbering on Sharon's knee.

Sharon envisioned the near future. It appeared to be an undifferentiated blackness. Emily sought to inject a bit of light. "I have an idea, Sharon," Emily began. "You are still a licensed financial advisor, are you not?"

"Yes," Sharon replied, "unfortunately one who has been discredited."

"Well, if you do nothing, the firm will assign your clients to other brokers. I suggest that you strike first. Write a letter of apology to each of your clients. Take responsibility for failed investments, but indicate that the failure was the result of unpredictable, once-in-a-lifetime disasters. Indicate that you will understand if they choose to terminate their relationship with you. But assure them that you always have had their best interests in mind. Promise to do better if they elect to retain your services. Hopefully, many clients will choose to remain. You could service their accounts from the study upstairs. Next year we will celebrate your success, and the demise of Sanderson Investments."

Max offered three barks of approval for Emily's plan. Sharon refilled her coffee mug. "It's worth a shot. Will you look over my letter to make sure it has the right tone?"

"Of course, whatever I can do to help," Emily replied.

Sharon ascended to the study. Max, Maude and Onyx waited patiently in the upstairs hallway for the closed study door to open.

At Home with Sharon

The animals' bowls had been filled. Emily dug into her granola. Sharon had not arrived yet in the kitchen. Emily arose to refill her coffee mug. At that point, Sharon entered the room. She yawned, scratched her left buttock, and collapsed into her assigned chair at the table. Sharon was still in her pajamas. Emily noted that the pink and white floral pattern appeared to clash with her brown hair.

"It was nice of you to get up to keep me company at breakfast," Emily declared with a hint of sarcasm.

Sharon scowled. "Well, there was no chance of an early-morning lie-in with you slamming bureau drawers," Sharon replied. "Remember, Emily, I will be hard at work today, even though I will not leave the house."

Emily looked down at the liquid in her coffee mug.

"C'mon, Emily, let's see some support here," Sharon pleaded. "I'm trying to survive in a cut-throat, male-dominated profession."

"I'm sorry," Emily said, instantly contrite. "You are right. We all are pulling for you." Max barked softly in support.

"How is the rescue operation going?" Emily asked.

"So far, so good," Sharon replied. "Six of my clients have called to say that they would remain with me. This afternoon two of my most important clients are coming here to discuss my plans for their investments."

The doorbell rang at two o'clock. Patricia Dolan was on time. Max, Maude and Onyx had been coached on proper behavior. Max barked once, just in case Sharon had not heard the bell. Pat greeted Sharon warmly. She then turned toward the assembled animals. Max extended his right paw. Pat shook it vigorously, scratching the area behind Max's ear with the fingers of her left hand.

Onyx arched her back and meowed for attention. Pat stroked the fur on her back. "What a beautiful cat," she exclaimed.

"We are friends for life," Onyx responded.

Sharon left Pat in the living room with the animals as she departed to prepare tea. Subsequently, the adults enjoyed oolong and biscuits. Pat was given treats to distribute to Max, Maude and Onyx.

"There is nothing like a tea party," Maude announced. The salmon-flavored treats had produced a most pleasant aftertaste. Maude leaped upon the sofa, looked at Pat, and decided to solicit some lap time. Pat responded with enthusiasm. She stroked Maude's fur as Sharon set forth an investment strategy for the near future.

Business concluded, Pat arose to leave. Max, Maude and Onyx provided a convoy to the front door. After Pat left, Sharon praised the animals for their contributions to the success of the interview.

Max, Maude and Onyx were in the backyard when the front doorbell rang again. Max sensed a possible violation of homestead security. He charged through the pet flap to investigate. When Max arrived in the living room, Sharon was in the process of welcoming Anna Samuels for a conference. Max sensed that Anna was a guest and not an intruder. He presented his right paw in a gesture of friendship. Anna shrank back, as if she suspected that Max had some evil intent.

Max was hurt by this rejection. Mrs. Samuels seemed to be a nice lady. However, she made it clear that she wanted nothing to do with him.

"It's not your fault, Max," Onyx said. "Don't take it personally. This lady is allergic to your dander."

"Dander? What is Dander?" Max asked. "I am quite certain I don't have any. Or is that another name for fleas? I have had fleas. They find my coat to be a great place to raise their families."

"Max," Onyx said, "your hair and skin give off scales that produce allergic reactions in some of our two-legged friends. These scales are referred to as 'dander.' The production of dander is a natural process. It is nothing about which to be ashamed. When you encounter a human being who is allergic to dander, you need to keep your distance. Some human beings even have an allergic reaction to us cats. Imagine that! It's crazy, I know, but some of our two-legged friends are deficient in this respect. We need to give people with allergies a great deal of space." Onyx led Max and Maude to their beds in the corner of the kitchen.

Anna was aware that she had offended the resident animals. She apologized profusely to Sharon. Sharon suggested that they move to her recently vacuumed study upstairs. She presented a plan to realize Anna's financial goals. Anna could not erase the image of Max's crestfallen face. She quickly accepted Sharon's plan. Anna resolved to communicate with Sharon exclusively over the internet in the future.

After Anna had departed, Sharon complimented Max, Maude and Onyx for their responsible behavior in difficult circumstances. "Thanks to you, I have secured my largest account," Sharon said, distributing a liver treat to Max and tuna-flavored treats to Maude and Onyx.

Max, Maude and Onyx met before bedtime to review the day's activities. "How do you like having Sharon at home with us during the week?" Onyx asked.

"It's great," Max replied, "I can alert Sharon to call the police if I discover a threat to homestead security."

"Good point, Max," Maude said, "But I see an opportunity here to enhance our standard of living. We need to find a way to get Sharon to make the mid-afternoon tea party a daily occurrence."

The Price of Gluttony

Emily and Sharon were in the kitchen preparing snacks. Max was sitting nearby. He was ranking the different types of snacks in order of interesting aromas. In addition, he was prepared to protect the kitchen floor from damage caused by snacks falling over the edge of the counter.

Maude and Onyx did not share Max's optimism about the possibility of falling snacks. They watched proceedings from the cat bed they shared.

"If only they would let me help," Max said to himself, "I could give valuable advice about the proportions of ingredients that make the best snacks. Unfortunately, I must wait until guests arrive before I can rank the snacks by taste."

Guests did arrive at six o'clock. The animals had been fed, in the hope that, appetites satisfied, they would not pester the guests.

Emily's brother Steve was the guest of honor at the party. Steve had gained control of his addictions to gambling and alcohol while attending the local community college. Earlier in the week he graduated with an Associate Degree in Hospitality Management from HCCC (Hamilton County Community College). Guests at the party included parents Donald and Fran Smith and friends from the college.

Sharon placed five trays on the dining room table. There was one tray each for pigs-in-blankets, shrimp balls, mini-pizzas, stuffed mushrooms, and assorted cheeses. Emily and Sharon assumed that guests would use the toothpicks on the table to spear desired snacks. However, Steve's college mates uniformly bypassed the toothpicks in favor of a combination of thumb and forefinger.

Onyx alerted Maude to this boorish behavior. "I dunno, Onyx," Maude replied, "in their defense, these are described sometimes as 'finger foods.'"

Max was having no luck in mooching snacks. Steve had warned his friends about Max's "paw-shake" routine. "Accept the paw, pet his head if you must, but don't give him any food," Steve instructed. "Max is a valued drug-detection dog. It is important that he keep fit."

"This is frustrating," Max said to himself. "All this food and no one will share." He left the living room, where his efforts to secure a snack had failed, and entered the dining room. Emily just had refilled the pigs-in-blankets tray. She had placed it near the edge of the table.

Max was overcome by the aroma. He stood on his back legs to get closer. He found that he could place his jaw over the edge of the tray. This orientation placed Max in a dilemma. He needed to remain upright to fully absorb the aroma of the fresh-out-of-the-oven pigs. However, this posture was very tiring. When he returned to all fours, he inadvertently brought the tray down off the table. There was a crash that interrupted conversations in the living room. Before Emily could intervene, Max had consumed two pigs.

Emily was furious. She dragged Max by his collar to the basement door. She opened it. Max descended the stairs to shouts of "Bad dog, Max".

This was the worst night Max could remember. With only a thin rug over a portion of the cement floor, he was most uncomfortable. Max whimpered during the remainder of the party. There was no response from upstairs. He tried a pleading bark or two and was told to shut up.

Max heard party goers leaving. "At last," he thought, "now I will be allowed back upstairs." However, the basement door remained closed. Max heard Emily and Sharon on clean-up duty in the kitchen. Then the front doorbell rang. Sharon again instructed Max to remain quiet.

Max caught the aroma of the lasagna that had been delivered. He pictured Sharon and the four Smiths at the dining room table, digging into that Italian delicacy. Max barked softly, hoping for forgiveness. He was told for the nth time to be quiet. Max spent a sleepless night waiting for morning.

Eventually it was morning. Sharon opened the basement door. Max was hungry, but he saw the look of disapproval on Sharon's face. He passed through the pet flap on the way to Polk Park.

As Max entered the park, he saw the legs of a toddler behind a bench to the right. He investigated. There indeed was a young child asleep on the grass, Max looked out into the park. A woman was trotting from one end to the other. Max heard cries of "William" as she glanced right and left. Max immediately made the connection. He approached the woman and performed his "dance in a circle while barking" routine. He then ran to the park bench and barked upon arrival. Mrs. Henderson followed him. Max pointed with his nose to the area behind the bench. Mother and child were reunited.

Mrs. Henderson thanked Max profusely. She wrote down the telephone number printed on his collar. She called Emily on her cell phone, expressing her gratitude for the insight of this wonderful dog, Max. Mrs. Henderson asked if she could drop off a bag of treats for him.

Mrs. Henderson was in the Smith-Grabowski kitchen when Max returned. He was greeted as a hero upon passing through the pet flap. He took note of his filled food bowl. He was hungry, but the attention he was receiving was too gratifying to pass up. His mood brightened further as Mrs. Henderson gushed over his intelligence. Max smiled modestly, accepted a liver treat, and excused himself to attend to the contents of his food bowl.

Onyx arrived to deliver a lecture on gluttony and self-restraint. Max nodded agreement as he moved from empty food bowl to water bowl. "Onyx is such a moralist," he muttered.

A Reality Check for Max

Max cornered Maude and Onyx at the base of the maple tree in the backyard. "I was standing alongside Officer Oliver at the airport today," he began. "I'm there to uncover drug dealers. Charlie then puts them in handcuffs. It is obvious which of us plays the more important role. Charlie never would apprehend a drug dealer without me. His senses are pathetic. It's my nose that makes the difference.

"Take today, for instance. A bag came onto the carousel. There was a strong aroma of ground coffee beans. I was instantly interested. Drug dealers often place cocaine packets inside bags of ground coffee. As the case passed beneath my nose, I discovered the underlying cocaine aroma.

"Now you might think that I would bark at this point. But that would alert the smuggler that I was on to him. He would abandon the bag and escape. Instead I stepped on Charlie's foot. This is our agreed-upon signal. Charlie bent down to scratch behind my ear. The smuggler was relieved. He believed that his bag had passed inspection by the all-knowing sniffer dog. I repeated the warning to Charlie the next time the bag passed. The smuggler, confident he had won the game, then swooped in to remove the bag from the carousel. Charlie got the collar and I received a promotion to 'sniffer dog, grade one.'"

Max paused to make sure that his audience was properly impressed by his achievement. Onyx had moved back a few feet and was gazing at the bird-feeder. Maude was grooming the fur on her front paws. Max appeared to be satisfied. He droned on. "That reminds me of the drug detection I made last month. Charlie had been warned to be on the lookout for a substantial shipment of drugs."

Maude and Onyx were saved for the time being by a call from Sharon. Dog food and cat food were ready for consumption in the kitchen.

After dinner, Onyx and Maude reviewed the day's activities. "Wow, another story from Max about his heroism at the airport," Onyx complained.

"Yes, he does seem to be fond of elaborating on his latest sniffing successes. Max has become a bit of a bore," Maude said.

Onyx took note of Maude's agreement. Without telling Maude, she planned a "reality check" for Max.

During the cocktail hour the next day, Onyx cornered Max. "I was talking with some of your mates at the park today, Max," she said.

"Oh," Max replied, who did you talk to?"

"Well, you know, I am terrible at names, and to speak frankly, you dogs all look alike to me."

"All alike?" Max responded with some irritation. "Surely you can see the difference between a St. Bernard and a dachshund."

"Well of course there are big dogs and small dogs," Onyx replied, "but they all are so 'dog-like.'"

"At any rate, your mates told me how proud they are of your accomplishments in the field of drug-detection. 'He is a credit to our species,' one of them said. 'A model for our youth,' said a second. A third dog pointed out that, although everyone has been impressed by one or another of your achievements, what is lacking is a presentation of the entire collection of your successful drug detections.

"He asked me to see if you would be willing to speak to them on this topic. There was a chorus of approval from the dogs present. I promised that you would address them tomorrow afternoon at four o'clock in Polk Park. I know that does not give you much time to prepare, but you are so good at speaking extemporaneously."

"Speaking what?" Max asked.

"Speaking freely and easily, without much deliberation," said Onyx with a smile.

"Oh, right, I am good at that," Max replied.

The next morning Onyx slipped out to the park. Fritz greeted her with a menacing growl.

"Cool it, Fritz," Zeno said. "This is Onyx. She lives with Max. She is under his protection."

"Sorry chief, I didn't know. It won't happen again," Fritz replied.

Onyx took Zeno aside. "Zeno," she whispered, "I heard a rumor that Angelo's Meat Market is holding a sausage-distribution event behind the store at four o'clock this afternoon. Apparently they made many more links than they could sell. I know it's on the opposite side of town, but they do make the best sausages. It would be best to be there early. Word does get around."

Onyx noted that her message had been well-received. Zeno and Fritz both had begun to drool. "Dogs," she thought, "what slobs they are."

Returning home, she asked Max how preparations for his speech were going. "All is well, Onyx. I have it under control. I will open with a joke about cats. You won't mind, I hope. Dogs love cat jokes.

"Why are dogs superior to cats?

"Because you can't get eight cats to pull a sled."

Onyx interrupted. "Why would a cat want to pull a sled?" she demanded.

"Relax, Onyx. Remember my audience. They all are dogs. They will appreciate the joke. I follow the joke with a straightforward description of five of my most important cases. I then conclude with a list of my commendations and promotions. The entire speech takes only fifty-six minutes. I will answer questions at the conclusion."

"Sounds good," Onyx said. "You will be leaving soon. Much as I would love to be there, it would be too risky for a cat to be in the audience. Maude and I will stay home. We look forward to your report about the event."

Max's subsequent report was succinct. "There was no event," he reported. "No one was there. Not a dog in sight. Did I go to the wrong place, Onyx?"

"No, Max. Polk Park was the agreed-upon location. And four o'clock today was the time selected."

"I anticipated a large crowd," Max said sadly, "I guess there's not much interest in learning about my achievements. At least I get respect at the police station and airport." He paused briefly. "And of course at home," he added, glancing at Onyx and Maude.

Onyx avoided the park for the next few weeks. She was afraid that some members of the Polk Park Pack might remember her role in spreading the false rumor about a sausage festival.

Max Gets Even

"Have you noticed that Max appears to be depressed lately, Onyx?" Maude asked.

"Well, he does seem to be preoccupied," Onyx replied. "I don't know why that should be."

"C'mon. You know perfectly well that he has figured out why there was no audience present in Polk Park to listen to his lecture about his many exploits. Zeno will have told him about the non-existent sausage festival. All the dogs in the park had left before Max arrived to deliver his speech. If I were you, I would be on the lookout for retribution. That may be why he appears to be preoccupied."

"But Max must realize how boring the stories about 'Max the Hero' had become. He needed a reality check."

"I'm not sure Max sees it that way," Maude replied.

Maude had given Onyx good advice. Max was looking for a suitable response to the mean trick Onyx had played on him. One afternoon he noticed that Maude and Onyx had very different reactions when Emily sprayed catnip oil on their scratching post. Maude was indifferent. "This is curious," he thought "Maude went into an extended session of screeching after eating catnip treats.* But she had no interest in the catnip spray on the scratching post. Onyx, however, appeared to be intoxicated." After scratching the post, she rolled on the rug in what Max took to be a state of extreme pleasure. Max filed this behavior in his memory for future use.

The next day Sharon and Emily arrived home from a trip to the Shady Acres Tree Farm. They dragged a freshly-cut specimen into the living room. It was destined to become fully decorated with lights, tinsel, and assorted ornaments, worthy to be saluted with a chorus of "O Tannenbaum."

At present, however, the tree reclined on its side on the living room rug as Emily and Sharon searched the garage for the Christmas tree stand. Max nosed open the cabinet door next to the sink in the kitchen. He removed the spray bottle of catnip oil, rolled it into the living room, removed the bottle cap with his teeth, and applied his paw to the plunger. The spray that emerged provided a substantial coating of catnip oil to the top of the tree. "This is excellent," Max said to himself as he re-capped the bottle and rolled it back to its place in the kitchen cabinet.

"I've found it," Sharon declared, as she liberated the tree stand from a collection of junk at the back of the garage. She and Emily wrestled the tree to an upright position and lifted it into the tree stand.

The tree was transformed during the next hour. Sharon turned on the lights and exchanged "oohs" and "ahs" with Emily. "We did a beautiful job, if I do say so myself," Sharon concluded. She and Emily retired to their bedroom upstairs.

Max watched from the kitchen doorway as Onyx caught the catnip-oil aroma. She sat in front of the tree, looking from side to side. She appeared to be in the process of calculating heights and distances. Calculations over, Onyx sprang up to the mantle over the fireplace, paused to assess the odds of reaching the top of the bookcase nearby, coiled her body, and leaped again. "Success," she declared to herself. At this height the aroma from the top of the tree was overpowering. Without giving it much thought, Onyx jumped from the bookcase. She embraced the catnip-flavored top branches of the tree.

What Onyx intended to be a hug turned out to be a blow. The tree came crashing down. Onyx was unhurt. She repeatedly rolled over a nearby upper branch, breaking the wings of a glass angel in the process.

Emily and Sharon responded quickly to the crash. They descended to the living room. Onyx appeared to be unconscious on the rug. Emily ran to the cat. "Are you all right?" she asked, stooping to pick her up.

Onyx slowly emerged from her catnip-high. She realized she was in Emily's lap on the living-room sofa.

"Perhaps there's a way out of this mess," she mused. "Emily seems to think that I was struck by the falling tree. Is it possible that she and Sharon will conclude that the tree fell over because it was not properly seated in its stand? Or just maybe they will blame Max. He is guilty of the occasional clumsy action."

Max arrived from sentry duty in the back yard. He stopped at his water bowl for liquid refreshment, and then entered the living room. Emily asked Max if he knew anything about the fall of the newly-decorated Christmas tree. Max responded with an innocent shrug. He then advanced to the tree top and delivered a number of noisy sniffs. He looked over at Emily to see if she had received the message. Emily ignored him. She continued to stroke the presumably frightened Onyx.

Max repeated the tree-sniffing, glancing at Sharon this time. "I think Max is trying to tell us something," Sharon said. She moved to the tree top, bent down, and imitated Max's sniffing routine.

"Emily, the tree top smells of mint, as well as pine. What do you suppose it is?" Sharon asked.

Emily joined the general sniffing activity. "I think it might be the catnip spray I bought for their scratching post," she said.

Sharon became lost in thought. She looked down at Onyx. Onyx feigned sleep. "Emily, I am beginning to see a scenario here," Sharon announced. "Only the top of the tree has the minty aroma. Suppose Onyx was attracted to this aroma. She could launch herself onto the treetop from the bookcase. Do you suppose she could leap from the mantle over the fireplace to the bookcase?"

Emily glanced from the bookcase to Onyx. "I'm sure she could," she said.

Onyx chose this moment to leave the living room for the sanctuary of her bed in the kitchen. Emily and Sharon took this to be an admission of guilt. They peered at the fallen tree with its numerous broken ornaments. Sharon then looked at Emily. "Basement?" she inquired.

"Basement, most definitely," Emily replied. Onyx was forcibly removed from her bed and placed upon the basement stairs. Sharon closed the door.

Passing through the kitchen, Emily noticed a smile on Max's face. "OK, Max, why are you in such a good mood?". Max replaced the smile with what he hoped would be taken as a look of innocence.

"Emily," Sharon said, "I think Max's delight at Onyx's banishment confirms our theory of the accident. There's one problem with our scenario, however. How did the treetop get saturated with catnip oil? I didn't notice any minty aroma on the tree when we brought it inside. Did you?"

"No, the tree just had the expected pine smell."

Emily opened the door of the cabinet next to the sink. "Aha," she observed, "the catnip spray bottle is resting on its side. I'm sure I placed it in an upright position after coating the scratching post. I suspect Max."

Max headed for the pet flap.

"Stay here, Max," Sharon commanded. Max stopped. He looked up at Emily, having adopted a self-righteous pose.

"Onyx deserves this punishment," he thought.

Emily and Sharon sat down at the kitchen table to decide what action, if any, to take.

"Unlike Onyx, Max is not a practical joker," Sharon observed. "He would not arrange this punishment for Onyx unless she had done something to deserve it."

"I agree," Emily replied, "I don't think we should punish Max. Let the animals settle their own problems."

Max was allowed a visit to the backyard. Onyx remained in the basement. There were no mice to hunt and no comfortable place to lie down. When Onyx protested her exile, she was told to shut up. Max and Maude spent a pleasant night curled up between Emily and Sharon on their bed.

* *Maude Smith-Grabowski, Diva.*

Black Cat Crossing

"Crossed any paths lately?" The question was addressed to Onyx by her friend Frieda, a sometimes visitor to the Smith-Grabowski backyard. Puzzled, Onyx asked Frieda, "What do you mean? Do you have particular paths in mind?"

"Onyx, surely you have heard the warning that when a black cat crosses your path, it brings bad luck."

"Really?" Onyx replied, "what kind of bad luck?"

"Well," Frieda replied, "the saying is not specific. But black cats are supposed to have the power to inflict injury or loss on those whose path they cross."

Onyx felt a surge of power spread through her body. It soon passed. Her normal skepticism returned. "So what happens if a person turns back and proceeds in the opposite direction when she sees a black cat run across the originally intended path?" Onyx asked.

"I don't know. It's an interesting question. Given your fur color, you are in a perfect position to accumulate data to answer it."

"You're right. Deliberate path-crossing might establish evidence of correlations of one type or another. Perhaps we could publish a paper on this topic in the *Journal of Experimental Psychology*." Frieda caught the sarcasm. She slinked off along the sidewalk.

Onyx returned to the kitchen. She was preoccupied with the "black-cat- crossing" adage. "One thing is clear," she thought, "the adage does not apply to owners of a black cat. I cross the paths of Emily and Sharon many times a day without anything bad happening to them. Perhaps the black cat that causes harm must be unknown to the person whose path is crossed."

Onyx expressed her concern about her "crossing power" to Max and Maude after dinner. Max was dismissive. "It's an old wives' tale," he declared. "It probably was invented by someone who had a grudge against black cats."

Maude took a different approach. "Let's take the 'black cat-crossing, subsequent harm' sequence to be an empirical claim. Onyx, you should put the claim to the test," she suggested.

The next morning Onyx took up a position beneath the shrubs facing the sidewalk. She spotted a young boy on a bicycle approaching from the right. Onyx checked for traffic, and then scampered across the sidewalk and road. The boy paid no attention.

Two houses past the Smith-Grabowski residence, his squeaking wheel awakened Nero, the resident pit bull. Nero was annoyed that his nap had been interrupted. He issued a menacing bark. The chain attached to his collar prevented pursuit, but the boy did not realize this. He lost control of the bicycle, skidding to a halt on the sidewalk. The subsequent screams suggested a life-threatening injury. Fortunately, the damage was restricted to a slightly scraped knee. The boy regained his feet. He limped off toward home, leaving behind his bicycle and that ferocious dog.

Onyx witnessed the boy's fall from the far side of the street. "Perhaps there is something to the old adage about black cats crossing," she thought. "If so, I possess great power."

Onyx was so self-absorbed that she didn't notice Maude's approach. "Why are you out here?" Maude asked.

"I am testing the 'black cat-crossing' hypothesis. So far the correlation appears to hold. I crossed the path of a boy on a bicycle and he had an accident shortly thereafter. Wait a minute, here comes a woman pushing a baby carriage."

Onyx once again confirmed the absence of cars on the road. Satisfied, she strolled to the other side of the street. The woman took note of this transit. She abruptly stopped the carriage and turned it around. There followed a collision with a five-year old girl on a tricycle. No harm was done, but cries emerged from both the carriage and the tricycle.

It was clear to Onyx that she had "black-cat power" regardless of whether the victim proceeded to cross her path or turned back instead. Maude remained skeptical. "Perhaps the woman remembered something she needed to do at home. The fact that you crossed her path may have been irrelevant."

"You're just upset because you don't have black fur," Onyx replied. "I have been given great power and I would be a fool not to exercise it."

Onyx recalled an incident that occurred when she was homeless and desperate for food. Midge Blakely had kicked her as she rummaged through the overturned Blakely garbage can. Onyx had crawled away in pain. Now it was time to right this wrong.

Onyx arrived at the Blakely house. She waited patiently. Soon Midge Blakely emerged from the front door, moving toward the car parked in the driveway. Onyx sprang into action. She ran at top speed between Midge and the car.

Midge jumped back, cursed, and then assumed a position behind the wheel of her car. Her adrenaline level was higher than normal. Shifting into reverse, she accelerated out of the driveway. The car's right rear wheel struck a toy truck that had been abandoned by Mikey, the six-year-old terror from next door. The truck flew off to the side of the driveway.

Maude had followed Onyx on her mission of revenge. She saw Onyx run between Midge and her car. Maude ran after Onyx to find out why she would do this. There occurred a collision between a flying toy truck and Maude.

Maude saw stars. The stars were replaced by a line of nine standing tablets. Written on the tablets were "life #1", "life #2", etc. The "life #1" tablet wobbled a bit and then stabilized.

Onyx heard Maude scream. She ran to her side, unaware that Maude had been following her. "Are you all right?" she asked.

"I'll be OK soon," Maude replied. "Does your 'black cat-crossing' correlation require that I be in pain?"

"Oh Maude, no, that was just an accident. It has nothing to do with the 'black cat-crossing' correlation. What is relevant is what happens to Midge Blakely."

"Most reassuring," Maude said. "I am going home."

After dinner, Maude called a meeting of the Smith-Grabowski animals. She addressed Onyx. "With great power comes great responsibility. You need to examine the results of your tests. I remind you that I almost lost one of my nine lives. I know this was not something you intended. But actions often have unintended consequences. You need to keep that in mind."

"I take your point, Maude," Onyx replied. "I've been thinking about this 'black cat-crossing' thing. Perhaps it is best not to cross any paths."

Max was frustrated by this discussion. "This is much ado about nothing," he declared. "It always is possible to find some event following a black cat-crossing that can be interpreted as unfavorable to the person whose path is crossed. One can defend the black -cat-crossing correlation in this way. But who cares?

"At any rate, a black cat crossing your path does not *cause* a harmful event to take place. What counts is the reaction of the person whose path is crossed. A rational person will say, 'That was a black cat running in front of me' and carry on as before. A superstitious person will say 'There goes a black cat, I'm in for it now.' The superstitious person then may alter her behavior in response to this irrational judgment. But this change of behavior is her choice. The cat is not responsible for it."

Onyx looked warmly at Max. "Thank you, Max, that is very reassuring."

Hollywood Beckons

The venerable law firm of Klinghofer, Cohen, Esposito and Smart was losing ground to the competition. Billable hours had declined by 20% in the last quarter. Kevin Esposito, Esq., attributed the decline to the success of advertising campaigns by competing law firms. "Just look at this," he commanded, placing a thumb drive in the computer connected to the room's television monitor. There followed a succession of messages that recently had saturated the Millwood airways:

> "Operation failed to cure your problem? You may be entitled to receive money for your pain and suffering. Contact Steve Schultz at the Schultz and Schultz law firm;"
>
> "Laid off from your job? You may have been discriminated against. Let Blakewell and Tong examine your case. We will sue to get your job back and obtain financial compensation from the company that fired you;"
>
> "Burdened by excessive taxes? Contact Klepper and Jones. We will search for perfectly legal remedies to reduce these taxes."

The other partners at the meeting agreed with Esposito. At some level they recognized that it was better for morale to blame outside forces for the firm's failure.

Esposito recommended a counter-attack. Klinghofer, et al., should enter the fray. Esposito announced that he had been in touch with the advertising firm Nothing But the Truth. "I know that 'ambulance chasing' is beneath contempt," he said. "We have never pursued such a strategy. However, times have changed and we need to place our name before the public."

Esposito had the complete attention of the partners. "NBT has pointed out that the ads of our competitors are not convincing," he said. "These ads fail to establish the professional status of the firm in question. In each case the spokesperson is a young woman who would not be out of place on a Victoria's Secret runway. NBT insists that messages from a prestigious firm such as Klinghofer, Cohen, Esposito and Smart should have more *gravitas*. Our messages should be in sharp contrast to ads from shysters whose spokespersons are bimbos who wouldn't know an affidavit if they tripped over one. NBT suggests that our case would be best presented by a woman active in the legal profession."

Max, Maude and Onyx joined Sharon in the kitchen as she prepared a pitcher of whisky sours. Max barked softly to remind her that whisky sours are best when served with snacks. "All right, Max, I haven't forgotten you." Sharon said. She spread pâté on several crackers and fish paste on others. Max barked approval and then ran to the garage door to welcome Emily.

Sharon carried the pitcher and two glasses as she accompanied Emily to the living room. The two women stretched out on the sofa. Sharon poured liquid into the glasses. "This will not do," Max thought. He rubbed his body across Sharon's legs. "Oh, sorry. I only have two hands." Sharon returned to the kitchen to bring back the tray of snacks.

Max surveyed the tray. There were four crackers of interest. Fish paste held no appeal. His instinct was to gulp down all four crackers at once. He realized, however, that such behavior might lead to exclusion from future snack-times. He sat patiently alongside the arm of the sofa, nudged Emily's arm with his nose, and accepted the cracker she handed him. "Life is good," Max thought as he anticipated three more deliveries.

"There was an interesting development at the firm today," Emily announced. "The partners have decided to advertise on local TV channels."

"Thank God. The viewing public has been waiting so long for this development," Sharon replied.

Emily ignored the sarcasm. "They decided to select as spokesperson a member of the firm," Emily said. She kicked off her shoes and flexed her toes. "They have chosen me."

Emily turned to Sharon to gauge her reaction.

"A perfect choice," Sharon said. "Who would have thought that those old geezers would realize that they were working with a future star of the big screen?"

Onyx indicated agreement by leaping from rug to sofa cushion to Emily's lap.

"A shooting has been scheduled for Monday. Will you help me rehearse my lines?" Emily asked.

"Of course," Sharon replied. There was a brief pause to refill empty glasses. Emily distributed the last of the snacks. "If I help you rehearse, and take charge of your wardrobe, can I be your agent?" Sharon asked in jest. "We could make this local gig a springboard to fame and fortune."

What Price Fame?

Sandro (Dro) Morelli spotted prey leaving the checkout counter. "Say, ain't you the Klinghofer babe? I seen you on Channel 4," he said with what he intended to be a seductive smile.

"Well, yes," Emily replied, seeking to express disinterest while remaining polite. Dro was oblivious to the implicit rejection.

"Babe, me and my roommate are having a rave Saturday night. You should come. I'll give you the address."

"I'm sorry, I can't," Emily said firmly.

"Babe, you can't miss this party. Manny Root will be there. Manny is an important director at Sunrise Pictures. He could make you a star," Dro urged.

"I'll bet," Emily said to herself. To Sandro she said "I'm just a hard-working paralegal. There are no stars in my eyes. Thank you just the same."

"Your loss, babe."

Maude and Onyx were on hand to provide direction, should that be required, as Sharon and Emily unloaded five bags containing groceries. Max was on drug-detection duty.

Sharon picked up a jar of peanut butter. "Emily," she complained, "I thought we agreed that the chunky version is best."

"I'm sorry, did I grab the wrong jar?" Emily replied. "I've had a bad week. Ever since the Klinghofer ad began to appear on TV, men have hit on me with varying degrees of crudity. I'm sure you must have encountered these displays of *machismo*. How do you deal with them?"

"My standard response is to smile and hit him sharply on the forearm with my fist. Then I say, 'Oh, that didn't hurt, did it?' The man will say 'Of course not.' Then I touch the same arm and say 'I'm sure you think that you're a stud, but you would have to grow a pair to interest me.' The usual response is 'That's not a problem, babe.' I then inform him that unfortunately he has the wrong kind of pair. If he is too dense to figure that out, I show him my can of pepper spray," Sharon declared.

"I could never do that," Emily said. "There must be another way to discourage them."

Before Sharon could suggest alternatives, Emily's cell phone rang.

"Emily Smith?" a male voice asked.

"Speaking," Emily replied.

"My name is Manny Root, Emily. You may have heard of me. Have you seen the movie 'Betrayed by Her Son'? . . . No? Well, I am the director of that highly-acclaimed film.

"The reason for my call is to see if you would be interested in auditioning for a major role in my new film 'The Innocence of Ends.' I have watched you perform in the Klinghofer ad. You have a natural screen presence. I think you would be perfect for the role of Diana in this film. Could we meet for dinner tonight to discuss this? I'll be returning to Hollywood early on Monday."

Emily allowed her mind to wander for a moment. "The award for best supporting actress goes to Emily Smith for her portrayal of Diana Fairborn in 'The Innocence of Ends'. . . But how likely is that? More likely, this Manny Root character is a slimeball looking to add another notch to his bedpost." Hands shaking slightly, she told Manny that she was anxious to discuss the role of Diana with him.

Over antipasti at D'Antonio's, Manny took Emily through the plot of 'The Innocence of Ends,' emphasizing the important contributions of Diana Fairborn. Emily was drawn to the narrative. Diana was a strong woman, much more than eye candy. However, she did not respond well to Manny's periodic touching of her arm for emphasis. She found Manny to be a persuasive conversationalist, but she was repelled by his piercing eyes, bald spot comb-over and presumption of physical familiarity.

Emily was guilty of consuming too much wine (an excellent Puligny-Montrachet) while she tried to resolve the tension between her distrust of Manny and her eagerness to buy into the role he had sketched for her.

Manny was pleased with developments. Emily was unsteady on her feet. She felt the need to take his arm on the way out of the restaurant.

Unknown to Manny and Emily, Sharon had decided to oversee their departure from D'Antonio's. She had brought with her the ultimate enforcer—Max.

Manny led Emily toward his car.

"This is not going to end well," Sharon thought. "Max, we need to bring Emily home with us," she said. Max was on high alert. When Sharon opened the car door, he made a straight-line charge at Manny. Manny, expressing his true nature, placed Emily between himself and this barking threat to his well-being.

Emily bent down and smothered Max in a bear-hug.

Max was confused. "What is my role here? Why the bear hug? And why do they call it a 'bear hug'?" he wondered. "Who, besides another bear, would want to hug a bear?"

Manny recognized the bond between Emily and this snarling canine. He relaxed. "Nice doggy," he ventured.

"Grr," Max responded, baring his teeth. Max placed himself defiantly between Emily and Manny.

Sharon arrived on the scene. Emily fell into her arms. Max barked three times, informing Manny that they were leaving and that any attempt to interfere would result in a call for an ambulance.

At home in the Smith-Grabowski kitchen, Sharon forced Emily to down a cup a black coffee. The animals grouped themselves around her, on the lookout for any snacks that might be forthcoming. Sharon made a fuss over the presentation of a dog biscuit to Max.

"Max," she said, "you put that phony director in his place." To Emily she said, "By the way, there is no such film as 'Betrayed by Her Son', and no record of anything directed by Manny Root."

"I am so ashamed," Emily said. "How could I have thought about leaving this house, even for a few weeks?"

"Meow'" said Maude and Onyx, echoing this sentiment.

Printed in Great Britain
by Amazon